Tales From Port Vic

Also by Margaret Bolton and published by Ginninderra Press
Not Another Nun Story
Mother & Son
Start with a Coffee (Pocket Poets)

Margaret Bolton

Tales From Port Vic

& other stories

Tales From Port Vic and other stories
ISBN 978 1 74027 944 4
Copyright © text Margaret Bolton 2015
Cover image: Margaret Bolton

First published 2015 by
GINNINDERRA PRESS
PO Box 3461 Port Adelaide 5015
www.ginninderrapress.com.au

Contents

Tales from Port Vic

My family lived at Port Victoria in the early 1950s from when I was seven until I was ten. Dad was the cop, whose territory encompassed Point Pearce Aboriginal Mission Station. As with many children of that age, I had a very fertile imagination and so these stories have elements of both truth and imagination in them.

April Fool

It was one of those grey, windy autumn days when thick clouds scudded across the sky before the wind, occasionally allowing the sun to check on the progress of things below, and the sea, grey too in sympathy, raised itself into short, sharp, choppy waves.

'Better take your coat to school. It might be raining by home time.' Mother was always in tune with the appropriate attire for the changing seasons. 'And be careful. Don't forget to keep your wits about you: it's April the first, you know.'

'What's so special about that?' Marg asked.

'It's a day when other people will try to trick you if you're not careful. It's called April Fool's Day.'

There were times when it seemed to the seven-year-old Marg that life was one big trick as far as other people were concerned. Off she went to school calling for her friend across the road on her way.

'Seen the ketch?' greeted Pat.

'No.'

'She's a beauty, a big two-master. It came in first thing this morning. It's tied up down at the jetty.'

'Oh,' replied Marg, without stopping to wonder how Pat had gained all this information so early in the morning. 'Let's walk down that street where you can see straight down to the jetty and get a good view. Hope she's still in after school so we can get a close look at her.'

Marg loved the sea, and with tales of her grandfather's sailing days ringing in her ears, she loved nothing more than to sit on a bollard at the jetty and watch a ketch being loaded or, even better, setting the canvas and sailing off beyond the reef to faraway places. 'Come on, let's hurry,' she called, leading the way.

'Ha ha, got you, you April Fool.' Pat danced with glee at her first victory for the day.

And after Mum had warned me and all, thought Marg as she continued dejectedly on her way, for Pat had gone off to join another group.

Suddenly near the church a gleaming in the grass caught Marg's eye and as she bent over she found it to be a two-shilling coin. It filled her with mixed feelings. Two shillings was more than she'd ever had before and already she'd mentally selected her favourite lollies at the corner shop further down the road. But in her heart she recalled previous reprimands about finding things that didn't belong. Father's position in the town didn't allow his eldest daughter to be spending money that wasn't hers for all the locals to see. In his eyes, the act of finding implied the consequence of leaving it there for its rightful owner to reclaim. And Mother never allowed lollies or cakes or biscuits – 'They'll ruin your teeth.' You'd think it was grandfather the dentist speaking, not a loving mother.

Finding it outside the church didn't help her decision either. God would know if no one else did and he would be displeased. Perhaps because it was a Church of England church and she not of that faith, he mightn't be so interested in her right then. Only the Catholic God kept his eye on her, and really this wasn't his territory. Or at least the Catholic God wouldn't think her an April Fool. So she pocketed the bright shiny coin and traded it at the shop for a whole bag full of many coloured and shaped confections, putting them in her case out of sight for safe-keeping.

The school morning began as always with the pupils perched on the array of dots on the asphalt beneath the flagpole. The dots were suitably spaced to allow an appropriate amount of room to raise the hands in salute to that bit of fluttering material that represented their country. This was followed by a rendering of the only two pieces they could play on their fifes: 'Oh Susannah' and 'John Brown's body'. The teachers too were probably blissfully unaware of the anomaly of those anthems with the flag. The wind wafted their shrill melody away leaving only a thin afterthought as they marched into their classrooms.

The morning passed quickly as the three Rs were given their rightful place at the prime of the day. In this field, Marg was the least of fools in that class. But recess time brought with it the inevitable Red Indians that flourished for a few weeks annually. Somehow the autumn winds brought out those primeval instincts in children that led the strongest to set out on whooping raids to ensnare and capture the weaker ones, leading them home to their tepees built of tall dried grass where the appropriate rituals of torture were administered. Hair pulling, poking, tickling and name calling were the order of the day.

Even the lollies wrenched from Marg's pockets were devoured by others. Never did she graduate from the ignominious prisoner in this game. Even Pat had managed to become the chief's first squaw – perhaps it was her long dark braids and tall lanky figure that earned her that position. Marg resigned her chubby self and her fair curly hair to their inevitable fate, but not without a longing in her heart for better things.

It was in the middle of the afternoon's poetry lesson when Marg had nearly finished her beautiful illustration of 'The windmill' in full flight, that suddenly and much to her dismay she felt a desperate call of nature coming on. How she hated having to put up her hand for permission to be excused and, with the toilets so far across the oval to the other side of the yard, much of the enjoyable part of the lesson would be missed.

'Watch out for magpies,' Pat whispered as she passed.

'Don't sit on a redback,' came another warning.

'The mother snake has had babies,' hissed the beady-eyed boy who had been the Indian chief inquisitor that morning.

The magpies Marg dismissed quickly, knowing that they only swooped in springtime to protect their nests. Still, she surveyed the tall grass carefully before setting out across the open space just in case they decided to join the day's conspiracy. Redbacks under the seat were an ever-present threat in those days when toilet facilities consisted of a wooden seat perched above a deep hole. Careful inspection with fingers to nose was a routine part of activities down there. None today – at least not visible – but who knows how many lurked in the dark and inaccessible corners of the holed bench.

But the snakes. She shuddered with the thought. Everyone knew that occasionally a brown snake took up residence on the covered ledge behind the toilet which acted as an air vent and as such was open to the long hole. And babies too, active little creatures, busily exploring their world. There would be no saying what they might do on encountering two fleshy little cheeks of a chubby bum, given the chance. Yet the beady-eyed boy too, might just have been adding to the day's fooling. Would she risk it? She really didn't have the time to contemplate all the factors necessary to decide whether the snakes were real or only April. But then again the venom of a brown snake was fatal, what about that!

Tears of anguish and frustration welled up and flowed forth and even crossed legs were of no avail. Running water everywhere. She couldn't possibly go back to the classroom. She slunk off home hoping that her mother would be too busy to notice that the hour was early. Perhaps she'd be able to sneak in the back door and Mum would be sewing in the dining room, preoccupied. She hoped that her father would be engrossed in his office and that no one would be leaving or entering the front door at that moment. She felt foolish enough as it was, without either of them adding to her anguish.

Suddenly a downpour of rain drenched her to the skin.

'Mum was right after all and my coat is still in my case at school,' Marg gasped and began to run. But then she realised the soaking rain would partly solve her problem, so she stopped, did a little pirouette on the spot with arms outstretched and face upturned to ensure a thorough soaking. Now only the problem of early arrival home had to be overcome.

She tiptoed down the drive, keeping to the grassy verge and off the telltale gravel as she passed under the window of her father's office.

As she crept in the door, her mother called out, 'Hello, dear! Had a good day? You're home early.'

'I got five early minutes,' Marg called back.

'You must have got caught in the rain. Are you wet?'

'I'm afraid I am.'

And as her mother came face to face, 'Oh, my goodness! You're soaking wet. Where's your coat?'

'The Red Indians took it!'

Jim, the Crim

He wasn't really a criminal, just a mischievous little boy, exploring his world like any other lively four-year-old.

He has always maintained that Grandma gave him the box of matches from above the stove and told him to light a fire. Perhaps…maybe…but it doesn't sound like the little old lady that I knew.

He lit his fire in two patches in the front garden. No lawns in those days, just dry grass growing in all the spaces not occupied by two circular garden beds with stone borders and two long thin rectangular beds bordering the fences. The grass was cut periodically, but not too often. It was quite long enough to easily get a little fire going. And that he did.

Mum was alerted by the smell of smoke and managed to extinguish it with the tap and a bucket while Grandma grabbed a couple of saucepans to help.

Jimmy got a thrashing and was told to never touch the matches in the kitchen again.

We had a simple bathroom – a wash basin, a bath, a chip heater, a cardboard box of chips and a cupboard that consisted of five wooden slatted packing cases stacked on top of each other with a curtain hanging across the front.

The matches were kept on the top shelf, quite accessible for lighting the chip heater and quite accessible to an enterprising kid. Well, she hadn't said anything about the matches in the bathroom, and really the front garden fire was a bit of a flop.

Surrounding our town on three sides was a golf course (the fourth side was the coastline). Nine holes with rough fairways and black scrapes, and fenced off from the road. Between the road and the fence was a wide verge of unmown grass, about four-feet high in midsummer. Do I need to elaborate further, except to say that in the absence of any sort of fire engine, it took most of the able-bodied men in the town to put it out.

Imagine the embarrassment that our father, the local cop, felt having to call in the townsfolk to extinguish the raging fire that his own son had started.

Needless to say, Jimmy was shoved in the backyard jail for the rest of the day, like any other common criminal. It was a small and poky cell with only a six-inch square door within the door for the policeman to see what the prisoner was up to. There was a hard wooden bench with a rough grey blanket folded neatly on the end, and an empty slops bucket that stunk.

Jimmy never took up arson again.

But he did get locked in jail on another occasion. He and his friend, Ivan the terrible, decided to make a cake in the chooks' water trough. They carefully mixed into the dough a couple of dozen eggs, some bran and pollard, a packet of feed pellets, a few globs of cod liver oil, a good dollop of chook shit and half a bag of cement. No recipe needed, just two cooks' combined intuition based on availability of ingredients.

'Come and see,' they regaled Mum. 'Come and see our beautiful cake.'

Dad was called out of his front room office to deal with something of this magnitude; after all, the chooks were his domain. He was not pleased.

Ivan was shouted at and sent home, while Jimmy copped a belting and ended up in the clink again. By the time he was let out, the concrete that he had wiped through his hair had set hard. He had to have all his beautiful fair curls cut off to be free of the rock-solid mess.

He does remember being locked in the jail once more, at Summertown, but he's forgotten what misdemeanour he'd committed. He was older by then and should have known better.

The Wreck of the *Albatross*

It was after sunset when they started. Harry had been so involved in policing the district that he'd not had a spare moment to build his chicken sheds, and now it was only twelve hours until the vulnerable little day-olds would arrive on the morning bus, packed in long flat boxes lined with straw. But as soon as he'd had his beer with the blokes at the pub (his way of supervising six o'clock closing) and snatched a quick sandwich, he started straight away.

He took Marg out to help him; she was the only one old enough. There were odd occasions when kids could be useful, even if only to hold the torch and pass the nails.

The wind was rising and heavy black clouds racing across the sky brought on a premature darkness. Out in the paddock on the edge of the town, man and daughter received the full force of each buffeting gust, directly off the sea, penetratingly cold. Marg shivered as she dutifully passed the nails one by one.

On the horizon, the lighthouse blurted out its periodic warning. The spray whipped up by the waves diffused its beam and occasionally the racing clouds blotted it out altogether. Marg was mesmerised by this irregular regularity to the extent that Harry had to speak sharply several times when the required nail wasn't there at the precise moment that it was needed.

'Come on, Marg, get with it,' he snapped. 'There's a storm brewing and we want to get finished before it gets here.'

'I heard about it on the wireless,' she replied. 'They said on the weather that the barometer was at a record low, whatever that means, and a storm warning is current.'

'I'm not at all surprised. Now let's get on with it. Hold that bloody torch properly.'

They continued working in a frantic silence, punctuated only by

Harry's swearing. Work wasn't work for him without the appropriate verbal accompaniment.

Gradually the whine of the wind began to rise in pitch, and the crash of breakers on the beach were echoes of those breaking on the reef further out.

Suddenly the rumble of thunder could be heard in the distance. Harry banged the iron sheets onto the wooden frames with increasing urgency, a job made more difficult by the wind's attempts to wrestle the sheets away from him.

'I can hear thunder, Dad. The storm must be getting closer.'

'Yes, and we've still got to get the iron onto two more sheds.'

'How many chickens in a shed, Dad?' Marg liked to know all the ins and outs of everything she did.

'About twenty.'

'Why can't they go in the big sheds with all the other hens?'

'They'd get bloody well trampled on or pecked to death. Day-old chicks are very small, just soft fluffy little balls of yellow down, and unless a hen is its mother, it wants nothing to do with the little buggers. You can imagine what four hundred hens would do to the tiny little things.'

'Why are you getting some more?'

'Some of the others are growing old and not laying as many eggs. It's not worth feeding them unless they lay every day. So the little ones will take their place and as they grow up we'll get rid of the old birds.'

'You mean Mum will have to chop their heads off?' Headless birds madly running their last circular race always upset Marg.

'Yes,' he grunted in reply.

Pity we couldn't have one for tea sometimes. That would make it all right. This thought Marg kept to herself, knowing that Harry's culinary tastes didn't extend to poultry, and that only at Christmas could such a treat be considered in financial terms.

As they continued battling the wind with their tools, the thunder got closer and flashes of lightning lit up the sky firstly on the horizon but soon erupting all around them. Marg was shivering uncontrollably, partly with the blasting cold but mostly in fear. The combination of darkness, thunder and lightning intensified her greatest fears; it was all that she could do to stay there without running home to the warmth of the wood stove and her mother's presence. But it would never do to admit cowardice in front of her father; that would incur a great wrath expressed in the most scathing of adjectives.

'It would be very frightening to be out there on a ship tonight. The sailors would be terrified.' It was all right to transfer her fears to some unidentifiable strangers. 'There's been a ship loading down at the jetty today. I wonder how it's going. It would be this sort of night that they get wrecked, wouldn't it?'

'Yes. Your grandfather was wrecked once.'

'Was he? Where? How? Tell me about it.' A good story was always welcome when recounted first-hand. It might even eclipse one's fears.

'It's not the time for stories now. We've got to get this done. Anyway, he didn't talk about it much. It was somewhere off the coast of Africa, some place called Nana Kroo.'

He must have been just like you, Marg thought. You only tell your good stories at celebrations when you've had a few. But just the thought of it gave Marg's imagination a boost. She could see it all in her mind's eye. She knew too that there'd often been ships wrecked out on the reef over the years. This little town had once been a major port where the really big sailing ships came to load wheat for the other side of the world. Some were too big to come into the jetty; they anchored out in the bay and were loaded by smaller boats. Even today, the occasional two-masted ketch came into port, and it was only just before the family moved in that the last of the deep-water boats, the *Passat*, had called. Grandpa the sailor would have been at home here in this town. Pity he died before he got a chance to visit.

Even now, she thought she could hear the scrunching and grinding of wood giving way to rocks from the direction of the reef, somewhat lost in the roar of waves but nevertheless unmistakable. 'Did you hear that, Dad?' she cried.

'What?'

'That noise like a ship getting grounded on the reef.'

'Don't be silly. You're letting your imagination run away with you again. Keep that torch straight.'

Marg found it hard to direct the torch's light properly with her head straining sideways trying to glimpse what might be going on out there.

Another flash of lightning lit up the whole sky. She was sure she could see the tall masts with flapping sails. There was a lot of foam where the cyclic motion of the waves was broken rudely by the reef, making it difficult to see clearly.

'It was, it was, I saw it!'

She was so excited that she beamed the torch shorewards, just as Harry's hammer was poised above the nail. It missed and got his finger.

'Bloody hell, now look what you've done. For Chrissake, Marg, shut up and get on with it.'

One didn't argue with this man who was both her father and the local policeman. It was easy for Marg to confuse his two roles, especially as her little brother had recently been punished by spending the afternoon in the lock-up. So she kept listening and casting furtive looks seaward as she tried to concentrate on the job in hand.

Suddenly an eerie glow lit up the sky. Even Harry couldn't fail to notice it.

'Look, look, Dad. What is it?' cried Marg.

'It appears to be some sort of signal. No, something's burning out there.'

The sails were very distinct now in this new light, ripped and shredded, and burning, one after another.

'The whole bloody ship will be alight soon. Guess I'd better go and do something about it.'

As they ran across the road and through the gate, they could hear the phone ringing insistently.

Mum came bursting through the door. 'It's for you, Harry. Some sort of emergency.'

As Marg stood by the fire trying to thaw out and straining to hear the one-sided conversation in the office, she indicated knowingly to her mother, 'It's a ship. And it's in trouble. I saw it first. Can I go with him?'

The thrill of excitement and desire to see this thing to its end was greater than Marg's innate fear. Besides, it would be all right. Her father would be near.

'It's cold and wet and late.' Eminently sensible, this mother of hers.

'Oh Mum, please!' she begged. 'Just this once. It's only eight o'clock now and I'll go to bed early tomorrow. Promise!' and she crossed her arms on her chest as a gesture of goodwill, but refrained from spitting in such company.

'All right. I'll ask Dad for you.'

For once, he must have shared her excitement, for he acquiesced with a gruff 'As long as you don't get in the way.' Perhaps it was because he'd revealed that tiny bit of his own childish disappointment about his Dad's reticence to share the excitement of his youth with his son.

They drove quickly down to the goods shed at the end of the jetty, where they met the harbour master.

'I've sent the pigeons across to the island with a message to send out their motor boat, and I've rung the owner of the launch here. He's going to get a couple of his fishermen mates and they'll go out,' he reported to Harry.

'It's bloody rough. Do you think it's safe to let them go? They could all end up in the drink.' Harry was aware of the risks for small boats when the sea was running so high.

'These blokes have had to do this sort of thing half their life. They know how to handle it.'

'If you say so.'

There really wasn't any alternative and it was clearly Harry's responsibility to do everything possible to save the crew.

Almost before he'd finished the sentence, the harbour master's mates turned up and put the boat in at the beach. It had been too rough to leave it moored in its usual place at the jetty. Most of the jetty was completely covered in water in a storm like this. Armed with blankets, ropes, lights and thermoses, the little launch soon disappeared from sight as it rounded the end of the jetty and headed out towards the reef, buffeted by heavy seas and drenched with spray as it went.

The waiting at the jetty seemed interminable. The three of them stamped around trying to keep warm, the men making small conversation to fill in the wondering gaps. It wasn't till both the boats returned that they got the story.

It was a ship that had been driven onto the reef and quickly began to break up. The water had rushed in through the holes, forcing the captain and his crew of three to climb up onto the charred yardarms of the masts to avoid being washed away. The crashing waves and moving hulk of the ship prevented the motor boats from drawing alongside. The fishermen yelled that they were going to make a series of runs past the sinking vessel and that one of the crew was to jump each time it passed. Their yells were half lost in the wind.

It took half a dozen runs to rescue the crew, but the captain wouldn't be in it. An old man, he was afraid and preferred to die in true seaman's tradition, going down with his ship rather than risk the broiling sea. The fishermen made several attempts to throw him a line before he could be persuaded that with it tied around his waist he could at least be pulled to the little boat safely.

By the time the two launches were returning to the jetty, the last of the *Albatross* was swallowed up and scrunched by the teeth of the sea.

Harry and the harbour master helped them all out of the boats when back at the beach and wrapped the soaked and terrified men in a fresh layer of blankets. Each of the land men then took one of the sea men home to spend the night. The captain went home with Harry and Marg to be warmed on the outside with a hot bath and crackling fire, and on the inside with Mum's scrambled egg specialty and Harry's Black Label.

Marg was sent to bed to dream dreams of excitement.

Next morning when the storm had blown itself out, she hurried down to the beach, for this was the time when the sea yielded up its best treasures for those who recognised them as such. She was an avid collector of shells.

Bits of wood, shreds of canvas, lengths of rope, iron bollards and pieces of anchor had been spewed onto the beach, along with pearly abalone shells, spidery volutes and fragile sunset-coloured scallops. But most prized of all were the shells the kids called 'ketches'.

A Curious Fowl Tale

A hundred years ago, Gilbert and Sullivan bemoaned that a policeman's lot was not a happy one. By the middle of last century, that situation hadn't changed much. A country cop had to provide his own car, not an easy task if you were in the habit of running them under trams on the occasional city visit. With three young children to feed and clothe, a policeman's wage didn't stretch to time payments on a car of the calibre necessary to stand up to high speeds on rough country roads and overloads of brawling drunks as passengers. So Dad took to selling eggs to raise a bit of extra cash (actually it was Mum who did the marketing).

Now, when my father went in for something, he did it in no small way. As you've probably guessed, in order to sell eggs, first you've got to have some chooks.

The police department owned the vacant corner block adjacent to our house, an ideal place to build chook houses. With his own bare hands and me passing nails, he erected suitable edifices complete with roosts, nests, food and water troughs to house four hundred of them. There was even a special grain storage shed to hold all their feed.

Egg collecting each day, wing clipping, dipping to kill ticks, gathering shell grit, getting broodies off, keeping at bay marauding enemies such as foxes, rats and snakes; these were all fowl activities. Mum's help was necessary for many of these tasks, while sorting, weighing, packaging for sale, Keep-egging for preservation and cooking our staple diet of scrambled eggs and sponge cakes with the cracked and soft-shelled ones were exclusively her domain. A child's place was definitely never within the egg precincts on pain of the strap or even jail.

This curious tale took place in the summer holidays on one of those hot dusty days when the north wind dries out adult nerve endings awfully quickly. Mum and Dad were both engaged in counting their flock. This involved letting them out of the shed into the yard one by one. Dad chased, Mum counted.

Suddenly a very angry face appeared over the fence yelling, 'Quick, Marg, get me the broomstick.'

When Dad spoke in that tone of voice, none of us children dared to question; instant obedience was called for. So I grabbed the broom handle (I didn't know why we kept this headless stick in the woodshed but this day its existence was justified). I passed it over the six-foot fence then listened in horror as Dad whack, whack, whacked around the chook house.

I cried for the poor little bantam rooster that sometimes flew into our fowl shed from a neighbouring house, no doubt seduced by so many females and a free feed. He was so pretty with his golden chest and bottle green tail feathers, but nothing made Dad more furious; he'd often threatened to 'have' him. At that time, being unaware of the fowl facts of life, I really couldn't understand why he had such a set against this delightful strutting creature and it upset me greatly to think that on this day Dad's fury had erupted into this senseless beating.

About ten minutes later, the sounds coming over the fence indicated that it was over, the battle was won; even a victory cheer could be heard. I couldn't empathise with it. As if to demonstrate his prowess, Dad threw the broomstick back over the fence. It landed, then curled up, no longer inanimate but lifeless.

I wondered what remained of the bantam that had been beaten so much that the broomstick now appeared distinctly snakelike.

The Chinaman

He came often to watch us at the playground. He passed it on his way home from work each day. We knew he lived in a very small cabin up the hill past the long line of caravans along the foreshore adjoining the playground. It was above the northern part of the beach which we seldom frequented. The striations in the rocky platform were deeply etched by a millennium of crashing waves making its surface formidable for our bare feet.

But the beach on the south side of the jetty was my favourite wandering place. I spent hours on my own with just the wind and the waves, looking for shells, seeing with my inner eye the sailing ships that I knew were wrecked on the reef, imagining all sorts of treasure safe down there in a watery world.

But the north side past the swimming area where the cabins were was a stretch where we just simply didn't go. It was shrouded in an air of mystery. What hideous creatures lived above that platform under the overhanging ledges, or dwelt in that cave whose mouth we didn't dare ever to approach? Mysterious, foreboding and full of danger.

It was on the headland above the cliff containing the cave that Lee Wong lived in his solitary cabin where the wind buffeted his window and spray from the breakers below showered his roof. What sort of man would live out there alone? Sure, in summer the other cabins housed families spending their holidays in our little town, but in winter it was a bleak and lonely place.

He came often to watch us at the playground. Standing there with his shining gold orb, rolling it lovingly in his delicate long fingers, just watching us silently through his slit eyes knowing that we would run off when he spoke in his high-pitched broken English.

Sometime he would offer us lollies, red and white bullseyes from a glass jar. But mostly he just stood there, his sleek black pigtail reaching down his back, and we just went on playing, keeping an eye on him just in case.

That gold ball had us intrigued. We invented all sorts of uses that he might have had for it. Did it give him some sort of sight into the future like its crystal counterpart? Maybe it contained opium which was burnt like incense in the crucible the priest used at church on special occasions. Perhaps it was solid gold and simply too precious to leave his person.

He came often to watch us at the playground, but no one had ever accepted his invitation to come over to his place. In a town like this, every kid knew that you never went with strangers. Some of the boys had once crept up to his window and looked in while he was away at work. They reported that there wasn't much inside, a wood stove with a large black cast-iron kettle on it, a simple table, a wooden crate for a chair, four more stacked crates for a cupboard and in the corner stood a plain iron bedstead with brass knobs on the corners. It had grey threadbare blankets and underneath was a huge black box.

This box quickly became another subject of curiosity and conjecture. Sometimes in summer when the sun danced and sparkled brightly on the waves, we imagined it to be full of gold. We'd learnt at school that there were many Chinese at the goldfields, but our grasp of the passage of time didn't inform us that that was at least a hundred years ago. We had no idea how old he was. His wrinkled sallow skin and shuffling gait suggested great antiquity, but his reported agility in handling two knives at once in the hotel kitchen where he worked suggested youth. We'd never seen another Chinese person to compare him with.

In winter when the mists that surrounded his headland were only penetrated by the incessant sweep of the lighthouse beam, we imagined the box to contain the skeleton of his wife, if he ever had one. Bleached and ghostly white, shrouded in red silk and locked in the black box, she must have died before any of us were born.

He came often to watch us at the playground. Sometimes the other children taunted him with childish insults about his yellow skin, slanty eyes and pigtail. He probably didn't really know what they were saying but, sensing the tone of voice, he'd turn and shuffle away along the dirt track, past the caravans and up the hill to his cabin.

I felt sorry for him: a kind of sympathy based on the knowledge that we were both loners. I often preferred my own company to that of those kids who would tease anyone who was in any way different. My spectacles and pre-adolescent chubbiness were often targets of their abuse too. And I just couldn't master the monkey bars. Four bars were all I could manage despite constant secret practice when no one was around. Often I'd sneak away to try again while the others were swimming or analysing a local fisherman's catch.

It was on one of those days as I dropped yet again to the ground from that fourth bar that I became aware of his silent sentinel. How long had he been watching? What had he seen in his golden ball while I was in mid-flight? On that day it had become a periscopic mirror.

'You likee de lolly, girlie?'

No one else was around, no one would see me, why not? And bullseyes were my favourite sweets.

'Thank you,' I whispered as I furtively approached the beckoning jar. As my hand reached in, I noticed the raised imprint pattern of flowers and berries on the glass. What beauty in such a mundane object.

'You likee de two?'

I hesitated, then quickly reached out for another one. A gentleness and understanding were emanating from his shiny face as he held out the jar, drawing me irresistibly.

'You like to come and see my house?'

At this moment, he seemed harmless. It was as if I were under his spell. In the back of my mind rose those images of him wielding his knives in agitation up at the hotel kitchen, and of that pearly white skeleton in the box under the bed. But I clearly relegated them to that hidden part of my consciousness, aware now only of his kind invitation and that soft lilt of his voice as I followed him past the caravans and up to the stark little house.

From deep in the folds of his high-collared gown he took a great black key attached to an umbilical chain and unlocked the door with great ceremony. First thing he did once inside was to stoke up the sleeping embers and put on the kettle. I was immediately at ease, for didn't my mother do exactly the same thing every time she walked in the door after even the briefest absence? I was expecting a nice hot cuppa to automatically follow, and wasn't disappointed.

'You like to drink tea?'

I nodded.

'It's very special tea, jasmine tea all the way from China.' It was the longest sentence I had ever heard him utter.

He perched me on his packing-case stool while he prepared the tea. From the very back of his packing-case cupboard with infinite care he withdrew a magnificent teapot and two darling little cups that matched. They had no handles and were the size and shape of standless eggcups. A golden-scaled dragon writhed around them beneath green-needled pines. Its fanged teeth imparted a fierceness which was belied by its sparkling eyes and colourful seaweed-like appendages as it romped among the flowers at the base of the pines.

Into the cups he poured a strange thin trickle of pale amber liquid, steaming with a mysterious fragrance. I watched him to see the proper way to drink it. With a reverence, he picked up the tiny cup in both hands and ever so slowly sipped the jasmine tea with his slanty eyes closed, savouring it all. I copied him, taken aback at first by how hot it was, and took a while to get used to the taste with no milk and sugar. He poured a second cup. By now I was beginning to like it and could even close my eyes like his.

Suddenly with a start I remembered the mysterious box and involuntarily turned to the bed to sneak a look. There it was right under the bed, as reported, but without an obvious aura of either gold or death. And it wasn't even black but a deep brown and, as my eyes became accustomed to the dark shadows of that corner, I could see that it had carvings on it.

Lee Wong noticed my interest. 'You like to see the box?' he asked invitingly and led me over.

I knelt on his oriental rug of deep maroon and indigo as he drew the box from under his bed. The delicate odour of the camphor wood pervaded the room as he pulled it into the middle. He raised the bamboo curtain of his window so that the light fell into a pool on the floor all around it.

Now I could clearly see the intricate carvings of a whole series of scenes dominated by a castellated, towered and arched wall, snaking across the hills with a bleak desolate country on one side and well-ordered green fields on the other. A kingly character was ordering three spear-carrying soldiers to capture a man making pottery jars and another weaving rushes into baskets. Some coolies in conical hats were planting rice in the background.

As I ran my hand over the surface, feeling the softness of the wood, I exclaimed excitedly, 'But my mother has one of these, just the same,' and she did. She'd got it on a trip to Hong Kong in the days of her wealth and freedom before she married my father. Her glory box, she'd always proudly explained. Nowadays she kept the blankets in it during the summer months. Our box had always had the distinctive odour of naphthalene that had hidden the mellow camphor wood odour that impregnated this one.

'I will tell you the story.' Lee Wong interrupted the thoughts of my mother.

By now I had become so attuned to his stilted tongue that it rang as perfect English to my ears.

'That man with the brass breastplate is the Emperor Shi Hwang-ti who built the Wall of Ten Thousand Miles to hold off Ghengis Khan and his hordes from Mongolia. Shi Hwang-ti believed that he was immortal, and pressed into service all sorts of able-bodied men for his protection. Potters, basket weavers, planters, reapers, all men had to have a turn as his bodyguard. Although he eventually did die, his name is still held sacred in the everlasting memorial of the Great Wall.'

I listened intently to this wondrous story but now my attention was drawn to the shiny gold latch. Mum's box of glory had a similar one but here was a difference; this one had a shiny gold padlock as well. I wondered if there was a shiny gold key in the depths of his robe to match it. Dare I ask him to open it? And if he did, could I bear to look inside?

Fear welled up inside me again. All the childish stories wove a fantastic web in my brain, a perfectly formed web but lacking the drops of dew that transform it into early morning jewellery. What if Lee Wong was really a big yellow spider with a black plaited streak across his back, disguised by his magic cloak of many faded colours? What if I was the fly, a fat, juicy, myopic fly, that had wandered unawares into his web?

An acute awareness of my serious transgression of being with a stranger overcame me. My inner depths urged me to go home to the safety of my mother's mantle, but my surface consciousness couldn't let me leave with this insatiable curiosity unabated.

I dared. 'What's inside?' I asked. Common sense didn't win that day.

'Aaah.' A long drawn out sigh and a small tear drop escaping over his high cheekbones. 'This is what I wanted to show you. Many years ago when I was a young man, I had a beautiful Chinese wife with ivory skin and long black hair shining like the moon. But she died as she was giving birth to our first-born son. The little creature couldn't face life without a mother and went to join her after only a few days. And now I'm getting old and don't know what to do with this box of hers that is so precious to me.'

He paused a minute while he slowly opened the box, and then one by one he laid at my feet all sorts of marvellous objects, each more wondrous than the last. There was an umbrella made of a paper-like material in a brilliant cerise with fantastic long-legged white birds flying against a radiating sun rising above an old gnarled tree branch. The ridge of the bamboo spokes that supported the shade was the sun's soul. A matching fan came next. The chopsticks were made of bamboo too, with tiny Chinese writings down the handle in a red dye. Several lengths of brilliantly embroidered material, one embossed with what seemed to be real gold, one a shiny silk in pure peacock, were followed by an outfit which I thought was pyjamas made of the softest, sheerest, pink floral bordered with red silk and gold piping. Some tiny orange blossom flowers on ribbons that he said were for her hair, and a jade-studded bracelet were lying on a bed of purple satin in a small intricately woven cane box with a tightly fitting lid.

Next came a box with hundreds of little tiles, each with shiny bamboo on the bottom and pictures and characters etched into ivory on the top, along with hundreds of small bamboo bones with sets of dots on the ends.

'Mah-jong,' he explained. 'If you come back sometime, I will show you how to play it.'

The other teacups from the dragon set that we'd used for our jasmine tea were nestled in among the materials, along with a beautiful vase of black shiny porcelain on which was painted an arrangement of chrysanthemums of all hues of gold, brown, purple and magenta with two gauzy-winged dragon flies passing by.

It seemed never ending. As Lee Wong stroked each of his wife's treasures, it was if he were fondling her. And last of all was a single faded photograph, taken when she was eighteen, he said.

'I want you to have them all. I've chosen you from all the young girls here. With your round rosy cheeks, golden curly hair and amethyst-blue eyes, you are as perfect for this country as she was for hers. It's all yours. Leave them in the box until the day you marry your beloved. They will cover you with glory too.'

He had indeed often come to watch us at the playground.

The Field Mouse and the House Mouse

Spring was in the air. The earth was beginning to warm up with new rays of sunshine, thin and wan at first, but gathering in intensity as the days grew longer. We youngsters stretched and yawned and got interested in life again. These recent spring rains had encouraged green shoots in the wheat field with the promise of summer plenty. Even the soil was moist and warm. All looked well in our world in the scrubby patch at the edge of the furthest paddock. All the women folk had recognised the signs and most were already pregnant. Our family numbers were about to explode.

*

A couple of months later on a hot summer's day when the green shoots had grown into golden grain, there came a knocking at the front of our house.

'Visitors, visitors,' I cried, and my ten kids all raced along our log and used their combined strength to move the chunk of wood that was our front door, just far enough to squeeze through one at a time behind me.

Blinking in the bright sunshine after the shade of inside, we were astonished to find a sleek fat mouse with long elegantly groomed whiskers, bright button eyes and great beads of sweat running down over his fat cheeks.

'Good morning to you. I'm your cousin Cecil, sent by my father to invite you all to the farm house for a while.'

'Come in, come in,' I cried. 'Sit yourself down and cool off. I'm Stan and these are Fred, Mabel, Vi, Ellie, the twins Bill and Gill, the little one is Marge, and this is the latest trio, Dorrie, Horrie and, oh dear, I can never remember the last one.'

'Morrie,' chimed the chorus.

'Oh, yes, Morrie. How silly of me. Now where was I? Come to your place? Well, we're really quite happy here. We lack nothing, the grain is ripe and there's plenty of it, although the way the population is growing I have my doubts about how it will keep us all going. Shoots and roots are a good standby, weed yams don't need much digging and the odd sour sob bulb comes to the surface. Even the amber resin oozing from the bark of these mallee trunks is still good. Why should we pack up and move holus bolus over there? Waste of time and energy if you ask me.'

Cecil sat up straight and put on a serious face. 'Mother is worried that since this great increase in population out here you'll all be hungry. She says that our house is large and full of nooks and crannies for you to stay in, and the pantry is well stocked, for Mrs Farmer is an excellent provider, not to mention Mr Farmer's grain store near the chicken shed.'

'Mmmm. I guess it could be worth a go. Things have been getting a bit dicey here lately, especially since Mr Farmer put in that huge trap thing. Tin sides it's got, four of them, with tops bent outwards. Right under the branches of the twelve-trunk tree he's put it, with hunks of cheese hanging just out of reach on their ends. Last week uncle Dave and cousin Jimmy were taken in by it. They fell off the branches trying to get the cheese, then couldn't get out of the square tin trap. Its shining sides stopped them from climbing out. Hundreds of mice have fallen in and then keeled over after eating the stuff on the floor inside. Lord knows what it is, but it gets them all right, and every morning Mr Farmer comes up with his wheelbarrow and carts the bodies away. But we've got more brains than to be sucked in by that thing. Yeah, I reckon we could give your house a go. Worth trying anyway. OK, you lot, get cracking, we're leaving as soon as the sun goes down. It'll be safer in the dark, I reckon.'

And so the tawny dusk found our whole family following Cecil to his house. Everywhere we looked there seemed to be similar processions heading in the same direction. Cecil showed us where his family was holed out and then led us to the pantry as if to prove his point. We were just getting through the cheese rind and the sugar bag and really hoeing in when I felt the stealthy swipe of a feline whicker.

'Quickly, scatter,' I cried as we all ran for cover.

That old tabby sat there for quite a while, his wicked eyes lit up by a shaft of moonlight coming through the small high window, but at last he gave up and slunk out. What a fright he gave us! Such monsters we didn't have at home; our attackers there had wings that flapped warning of their approach. Some hooted, others laughed.

When our hearts had stopped pounding and our knees had stopped knocking, I decided enough was enough and insisted on retiring. We were full anyway and any more scares like that would give a bloke a heart attack. Safely in the hole, we had a roll call. Two were missing.

'Anyone seen Mabel and Vi?' I asked.

'Nooo,' chimed the chorus.

'Hang on a minute,' Bill piped up. 'I reckon I saw them eating cheese with all those strangers in the upside down wire netting basin.'

'Oh dear,' Cecil cried, 'I'm afraid that thing is a trap. Once you go down the cone, there's no way of getting out.'

'Oh Lord,' I said. 'What a contraption.'

But worse was yet to come.

Next day when Cecil took us down to the grain store, there seemed to be no end to moving bodies of mice. I'd never dreamed that so many mice even existed, let alone all at this one house. There was indeed plenty to eat in the grain shed. Every bag of wheat had holes bitten into it, with grain spilling out like Niagara Falls. We all ate our fill despite constant jostling on all sides.

Suddenly the air was rent with high-pitched squeaks. Human children were coming! We all rushed for cover, but where to? Every space was occupied four times over. Even the boards to which the sides of the shed were nailed were covered with brown furry bodies, tails hanging over the edge like soldiers lined up for inspection. I watched in fear as the children grabbed handfuls of tails and ran out in glee, the dozen mice in each hand writhing like contortionists, their writhings turning into death throes as they were dumped in the incinerator. What a game! And here they were back for more. I managed to escape through a crack in the back of the shed and headed for the woodshed hoping to find it quieter.

This was nearly the end of me. I saw the cheese stuck in the mouth of a horizontal bottle, ran out to it over the bag-covered part onto the neck. Too late I realised that the neck of the bottle was bare, and felt myself slipping, falling into an unknown fate below. A kerosene tin of water was waiting to envelope me in its folds, but luck was with me once again. So full was the bucket of drowned mice that I could run around on the corpses floating on the top without even getting my feet wet.

And Cecil recommended this life!

I'd had enough. Jumping out, I quickly began to search for my children. In this milling mob, it was impossible.

Suddenly Bill and Gill whizzed past, so I grabbed them.

'Seen the others?'

'Yeah, Marge and the trio are still in the grain shed.'

'You go and get them while I look for Fred and Ellie. Meet you at the front gate in five minutes. We're going home while we can. Whoever imagined that things could be better here just because of more food? Better to be a bit hungry at home than half dead here. Let's go!'

Family Stories

The first four of these stories are from my own family history, while the last two are of the family of friends.

With thanks to Diane Hunt and Paul and Margaret Emery for sharing with me their stories of Charlie Patterson's diary and the art of celery growing.

Trees and Chooks – A Triptych

The Peppercorn Tree

Our house at Sedan had a pepper tree in the yard with lots of knobbly little peppercorns that hung like branches of grapes with thin pink paper coverings on them.

We lived opposite Laucke's flour mill. When the wind blew from the north, the dust was red or brown, and thick, but when it was from the west, the dust was white and fine, like the powder that Mummy put on my baby brother's botty and thingy.

We had a few chooks that lived in a tin chook house not far from the pepper tree. They were often allowed to run free around the paddock, but never allowed over the fence into the back garden. Sometimes, though, they flew over; then Dad would clip their wings. They spent their time just pecking around, looking for worms and weeds and squawking long slow squawks, with their tails held high and their red combs flopping about. White chooks laid white eggs and black chooks laid brown eggs that Mummy always said were more nutritious (that means better for you).

Christine, who lived on the other side of the paddock, often had chickens but our chooks never laid chickens. We had lots of eggs but no chickens ever came out. Still, I looked carefully every time Mum cut the top off a boiled egg at breakfast time, just in case. I liked chickens – little soft and fluffy squeaky things that never sat still.

I often asked Mum why we never had any chickens. She always had the same answer: 'Because we don't have a rooster.' I came to think that chooks laid breakfast eggs and roosters laid chicken eggs.

I got to see a chicken in an egg once. One of Christine's chooks was sitting on a nest in the woodpile on her side of the paddock. She reckoned that the eggs had chickens hatching in them, but I didn't believe her because I could see that it was a chook, not a rooster, sitting on the eggs. So I had to see who was right. I didn't feel good about throwing the rock into the nest, but Christine said it would be OK, even though she wouldn't do it. And I felt even worse afterwards because it died, that not-yet-chicken but a blob with sticking-out eyes. It did have a beak, though.

My little sister and I played a lot under the pepper tree. I was the mother and she and her Minnie (that funny flop-eared thing she lugged around all the time) and the chooks were the kids.

The long and thick hanging branches of the pepper tree were the walls of our house; the spaces between them were the doors and windows. I made mud pies and decorated them with pink peppercorns, and was disappointed when my sister stirred them up instead of eating them. And she made such a mess all over her fingers and clothes and on the floor of my house.

And guess who was the one who got into trouble about the messy clothes? No, it wasn't my sister; she was too young to think up such naughtiness, and I was bad for 'leading her astray'.

After I started school, we stopped playing houses and started playing schools. I taught her more useful things like counting and reading. The chooks had been all right as children but were no good as students. It was OK not to listen when the mother shouted at them, but you just can't do that sort of thing at school, so we shooed them out of the pepper tree classroom.

The Tamarisk Tree

Our house at Port Vic had a line of scrawny tamarisks along the back fence with branches that could whip you if you weren't careful. In the spring, it had flowers that were the same dirty pink colour as the satin petticoats that often hung on the line of the lady who lived over the back fence. You could see her geese too if you were up the tamarisk tree.

We lived a couple of blocks back from the seashore and on stormy nights we could hear the waves crashing and the thunder roaring. Sometimes it was the thunder that crashed and the waves that roared.

We had chooks by the millions at this place. They came in flat boxes on the bus as day-old chicks and lived on the vacant block next door in a row of proper chook houses with wire fronts, iron perches, concrete water troughs and wooden nests to lay their eggs in. All mod cons.

Dad looked after the chooks. He fed them, checked the bobble in the water trough, dipped them to kill the lice, clipped their wings to stop them flying away, cleaned the sheds and kept count that none of the four hundred got away.

Mum looked after the eggs. She collected them, cleaned and graded them, rubbed them with Keep-egg, and packed them for sale. We had eggs for breakfast, lunch and tea, and sponge cakes in between, for Mum cooked all the broken and soft-shelled ones that couldn't be sold. For at this place, the chooks brought us money. Country cops had to buy their own car and Dad had driven ours into the back of a tram in the city just before we moved to Port Vic.

My sister got asthma from all the feathers, dust and bugs. She also got lots of special treatment because of this and never had to dry the dishes or set the table.

One of the tamarisks became our favourite – the acrobat tree. Swinging upside down like a bat flapping in the breeze, with skirts hanging down over our heads and homemade undies showing. The rush of blood to the head and competition about new abilities were exciting.

The tamarisk tree was right outside the lavvy door. You could sit with the door open and legs dangling and imagine the tree to be everything else but a tree. The lavvy was perched over a long drop, into which Mum sometimes threw an old saucepan of lime. The smell of the lime swamped the other, but made me think of the hellfire and damnation that we sometimes heard about at church.

The lavvy was a place of learning as well as dreaming. Hanging on a string from a nail on the wooden frame were cut-up squares of the daily newspaper provided for wiping. The things I learnt from my morning's read were never mentioned at school and seldom at home. I also learnt about white lies, for we had to 'do one' every morning before we went to school.

You had to be careful how you sat on the lavvy because the hole in the seat was made for grown-ups and kids could fall through if you weren't too careful. I reckoned it would be like quicksand down there – you could get sucked under with a silent gloomp and be gone forever. Well, that's how it was with my friend Marie's patent leather shoes that she had placed under the tamarisk tree while having her turn at showing what she could do. My little brother quickly got hold of them and chucked them down the hole. Some of the egg money that week went into buying new shoes.

On the other side of the lavvy was the jail. You could tell how important a country police station was by the number of cells in the backyard. We only had one but it was regularly occupied by several Aborigines. If more than four had to stay overnight, Dad had to take the extras to the next town. They could be noisy at night but were always very friendly when sober the next day. We had to play in the front yard or at other kids' places when there were prisoners in the backyard. And Mum often killed a chook to feed prisoners, but we only had chook to eat on Christmas Day.

The chopping block for chooks and the copper for dunking-before-plucking were next to our tamarisks. Great was the day when the chook got away without its head and ran madly around in smaller and smaller circles until it dropped dead.

My little brother got locked in the jail a couple of times. The longest time was when he and his mate had mixed a giant cake in the water trough in the chook yard using dozens of eggs and a bag of cement. His mate only got a telling off even though Mum reckoned he was the ringleader.

The Pine Tree

Our house at Summertown had a humungous backyard that went all the way down the hill. On either side, there was a flanking row of old, tall and gnarly pine trees that were great for climbing. It took a lot of concentration and angular contortion to get to the top, but once there the view of the whole valley of market gardens was spectacular.

We lived on the main road through the hills, opposite a cemetery that we weren't allowed to frequent.

With such a big yard, we just had to have a vegie garden and some chooks, but not too many this time. And it was my misfortune to feed and water them both morning and night, whatever the weather, and to collect the eggs. Their shed was under a pine tree about halfway down the long hill with steps going down to it. A long way when it was hailing or pouring with rain, which it did all winter.

One damp and foggy morning in a fit of adolescent angst, I chucked the whole bucket of water at my mother as I set out on the dreaded journey down the steps. Needless to say, she was not pleased.

On the same evening, I tripped on the return journey with the eggs, with breaking consequences. My mother reckoned I did it on purpose. It was a long time before we were speaking again.

Yeah, trees (and my mother) are still my friends, but not chooks any more. My mother even got me this brand-new baby brother just before we moved to Portagutta.

Three Sailing Ships On My Family Tree

Ganymede

Way out on a far limb of the family tree lived a master mariner, William Thomas Brown and his wife, Mary Josephine, from Liverpool in England. William took his pregnant wife on the long journey to South Australia when he captained the *Ganymede*, a three-masted, 167-foot iron barque of 569 tons.

On April Fool's day in 1879 while loading wheat at the Queen's Wharf at Port Pirie to take back to the UK, the *Ganymede* caught fire. A kerosene lantern was tipped over in the lazarette, a small storeroom below deck in the aft of the ship. The flames quickly licked the floorboards, then breaking through the deck, leapt high into the air and consumed the timbers. Acrid smoke billowed profusely. William and Mary Josephine ran for their life down the gangplank, leaving behind everything they had brought with them. They left so quickly that Mary Josephine didn't even time to put on her hat. She lost all her clothes and some precious jewellery. The ship was quickly manoeuvred into midstream, but neighbouring boats had difficulty putting out the fire. Eventually the flames were quelled, and a tugboat towed the gutted ship all the way to the slipway of Henry Fletcher's yard in Port Adelaide, where she was repaired to sea worthiness again at the cost of £2,000.

But the whole ordeal was too much for Mary Josephine. Her contractions came early. William had hoped to be back at Liverpool before the baby was born. She delivered a tiny little girl and called her Adelaide in honour of her birthplace. It was touch and go for a while, so premature was she. This child would certainly never be allowed to forget her untimely birth in a far away, strange place.

It would take many months to rebuild the *Ganymede* at Port Adelaide, so Henry Fletcher bought it, and the Brown family made their way back to England on a passenger ship. Needless to say, Mary Josephine never again sailed with her husband.

Glenogil

Much nearer to the centre of the family tree – in fact, sitting right on the trunk – was my German grandfather, Heinrich Simon Breuer. He was an able seaman in the British merchant navy when in June 1910 he visited Port Adelaide in the *Glenogil*. She was a four-masted steel barque rigged with royal sails over double top and single topgallant sails. At 278 feet long and weighing in at 2,285 tons gross, she was much bigger than the *Ganymede*. Sailing round the world from Europe to Sydney and back to Liverpool via the Horn, she stopped at Adelaide to take on a load of wheat.

At daybreak on the third day in port, the day that the ship was to sail out of Port Adelaide, a day which was cold with an overcast sky, Heinrich, or Harry as the other sailors called him, was furtively stowing his clothes in his bag. He was jumping ship. Five others also left this ship on this trip at this port. Perhaps the captain was unreasonable in his demands, or perhaps the cook hopeless, too often burning the salt meat and pantiles that were on the sailing menu. The trouble with deserting was that a sailor forfeited the pay due to him. He also had to leave behind his certificate of continuous discharge that was virtually his passport to further employment. Above all, it was considered a punishable offence to desert one's ship; he could be arrested.

Hoping for the best, Harry put on his duffel coat with a few coins in his pocket, but he left behind his oilskins and thigh-high Wellingtons, and stealthily crept down the gangplank. He liked the look of this country. He had called in at Port Adelaide four years earlier and spent some time wandering the streets and imbibing life in this city. A man could live a good life here. He caught the train taking early morning workers into the city, then headed for the distant blue hills on foot.

Alert

Some thirty years after jumping ship at Port Adelaide, Harry Breuer found himself stalking the wharves again. He was looking for work. He had spent the intervening years unsuccessfully share-farming for a politician in the mallee country, country where droughts, dust storms and low wheat prices brought a man and his family low, and depression forced many off the land and into the city. Not that the city offered a failed wheat farmer any employment.

He found a ketch that was looking for a deck hand and he jumped at the chance. The *Alert* was a small coastal trading vessel, with two masts and sails for when the wind was up and a twin-screw auxiliary engine for when the wind was absent. Only 70 feet long and of 45 tons, it carried stores from its base at Port Adelaide to small country ports and picked up wheat or salt for the return trip.

Loading wheat was difficult for Harry, who was getting on in years by this time. Bags of wheat were handed down to him in the hold, balanced on the canvas cloth on his shoulder and then manoeuvred with a bag hook. Unable to stand straight in the small hold, his back ached a lot. The load had to be positioned evenly on each side and in such a manner that it wouldn't shift in big seas.

Harry was also the cook. In the minuscule galley, cooking wasn't difficult as long as the fire in the stove could be kept alight. Often, fresh food and meat could be picked up at ports; fish were easy to catch.

A small cramped bunk had only a kerosene lamp to light the cold night watches. A bucket of water heated on the galley stove provided washing facilities of sorts, while pissing over the side obviated the necessity for a toilet.

By the end of World War II, with its petrol rationing and the rise of road transport, the number of ketches diminished greatly. Soon Harry would move on to larger interstate steamers.

The *Alert* came to an inglorious end. In 1960 she was beached in the mud at the ships' graveyard at Mangrove Cove on the western edge of the Port River just north of the railway bridge. Here she was gradually broken up by Robert Gregory. But Robert was a slow worker and the demolition deemed unsatisfactory, so she was burnt to the waterline. Robert Gregory's inability to meet the conditions of the breaking-up contract led to a three-month stint in the clink.

And so now the *Alert* lies amouldering in her muddy grave. The mud stinks at low tide. A few seagulls squawk around looking for a snack in the mud. There is not much left of her but rotting wooden planks and a few rusty screws. Just the centreboard casing protrudes above the mud. Mangroves have grown around her so that even what is left is hardly visible. Nowadays there is an interpretive sign pointing to where she lies. But nothing else to show what a great little ketch she once was, based at Port Adelaide and working the coastal ports of South Australian waters.

Henry Bolton: The Foot Man

Hailing from Yorkshire, seven-year-old Henry Bolton, the baby of the family, came to Australia in 1883 with his parents, two of his brothers and his sister. Two older brothers had arrived a year earlier. The family disembarked in Brisbane but, before two years were out, moved to Sydney. Perhaps the weather was too warm for them.

When Henry left school, he was apprenticed to a bootmaker for four years. He worked as a boot clicker – he put holes into leather boots for the laces go through. Sometimes Henry was a labourer and sometimes he was a swagman roaming the country, purportedly searching for work, but really just seeing Australia and enjoying the experience and the handouts that people gave him.

Once, Henry had to jump to save his life. He jumped from a thirty-foot-high window and broke both his ankles. Taken to the Royal Prince Alfred Hospital, he was off work for five months while the ankles mended. He returned to his work of clicking, for at least you could sit down on the job.

Three years later, when World War I broke out, he enlisted in the army. Henry was thirty-nine at the time, but told the army he was only thirty-six. It wasn't that he was all that patriotic for his new land, it was more that the army represented a steady job with dependable pay. Bugger the danger. The mateship was good too.

After two months' training, he sailed to Gallipoli as part of the 45th Battalion. He had done no route marching during his training period, but after five and a half months at Anzac Cove, route marching caused trouble with his legs and feet and he had to be carried. He had suddenly developed cramping calf muscles with pain in his ankles, and the condition was getting worse. He was also short-winded when marching. He found himself in hospital in early 1916 at Ghezirah in Egypt with fractured ankles again. While there, he went on a couple of benders, returning to the camp late, and so was slapped with an AWOL charge and confined to barracks for a short period each time.

By the middle of June 1916, Henry was in France, where he was allocated to base duties. Even so, the constant barrage of nearby gunfire assaulted his ears, the smell of explosives and death made him chunder and his feet pained him greatly. In response to all this, he found himself pissing his pants every hour or so during both day and night. After less than a year in France, he spent a short period in hospital in England before they sent him home again. He was discharged as medically unfit.

A year later, with still no job to get up for every day, Henry re-enlisted in the army and worked at the concentration camp south of Sydney guarding the interned Germans, but that only lasted a week. Too much footwork in guarding the perimeter fences. So he applied for a war pension to see him through.

In Sydney, he lived near enough to his mum to be able to go home for a Sunday roast each week. But he never found a wife, for he couldn't take girls dancing. He ended up in the TB sanatorium at Waterfall, filled with consumption like his father before him.

He died single and a lonely man, but glad to put his feet up at last.

Beauty

I could hear the other horses snorting around in their stalls, clearing their nasal passages, tossing their heads, stamping their feet, trying to warm up – the usual waking-up routine. Outside, it was still dark, the sky just beginning to show its pale lilac light in the east, the frost an inch thick on the ground.

It wasn't long before Henry turned up to get us ready for the day's work. 'Hi ho, my beauties,' he said.

It was always the same: you could hear the love in his voice, but also the awe, for we were big drafties – I'm a seventeen-hand grey, wide across the chest, and my hooves can pack a punch if need be. I can fit four boys on my back, no trouble at all.

'Time to front up for work, my hearties.' Despite its softness, Henry's young voice was authoritative. 'A quick groom, some tucker, then off you go. Dad will be here in no time to harness you up to the plough.'

There was something very pleasurable in the grooming for an old horse. First the curry comb in wide circles got rid of the sand and dirt, then the dandy brush got the tangles out of my mane and tail, followed by a soft brush for my face and legs. Lastly my hooves were checked to make sure no three-cornered jacks or stones had got stuck there.

'Good girl, my big Beauty,' Henry crooned. A pat on the rump signalled that he'd finished with me, then he moved on to the next horse. Six of us lived at the Breuers'.

Then my favourite breakfast, bran and hay, followed by a long draught of tank water as the pipes were frozen solid at this time of the morning.

Being old has some advantages. I no longer work in the paddocks, pulling ploughs and reapers in a team of four. I am the school horse. So I have to wait a bit before the boys set out on our daily journey.

After he'd had his own breakfast of boiled wheat and stale bread toast with jam, Henry harnessed me to the small wagon that carried the three of them to school. First the bit and bridle, then the shafts and lastly the reins. I always resisted the bit. Nasty piece of work that – it often hurt my mouth.

Always boisterous and laughing, Claude and Alan liked to outdo each other in daring deeds. It was a good thing that Henry wouldn't allow them to take the reins very often, for I might have buckled under the pressure of their antics. Sometimes they loaded an old kero tin with a fire in it to keep warm. I had to provide a smooth ride on those mornings.

One day, it did tip over, and burnt a small hole in the floor of the wagon before the boys could extinguish it with sand, for the six-mile road to school was very sandy. It made pulling the cart hard work. Their dad was very angry about the hole in the wagon floor and the boys copped a hiding.

On the way, we stopped to pick up the two Symons girls. Henry gave them his most charming attention and was twice as bossy with his brothers in the presence of the girls.

School was held in the Nadda town hall, not as fancy as it sounds. It was the only building in the place besides one large house, and a lavatory on the railway siding. Lots of kids came on horses, so when we were all tied up within reach of the water trough, chaff bags around our neck, we could at least idle away the boredom of waiting all day for the homeward trip by gossiping among ourselves. The kids came to offer crusts, apples and pats at lunchtime, and some tried to mount us. I always shook them off, for they could be very rough at times, grabbing a mane to pull themselves up and then shouting something about being the king of the castle.

Then home again at the end of school. Not my favourite time of the day, for the kids liked to let off steam by having races with other wagons and carts, belting me with the reins to make me go faster. It was near impossible to speed on the sandy track. Those show-off Wishart kids, imagining they were charioteers in their fancy light trap, would of course always win. How I pitied their fine roan.

So at times, retirement is only marginally better than working. Don't know how much longer I can carry on with this caper, but at least I'm appreciated by Henry.

Charles Patterson's Diary

Charles Patterson kept a terse diary for nearly four years.

In 1904, Charlie Patterson travelled by horse and wagon from Port Pirie up to Port Augusta and then south past Whyalla to live on and work his newly gotten piece of land. He took a workmate and a dog with him but the dog ate a poisonous bait on the way and that was it for the dog. The land was barren but covered in scrubby bushes and mallee.

Charlie had a couple of ketches, the *Wilpena* and the *Phoebe*, on which he planned to send firewood and posts across the gulf to Port Pirie, where his sons would sell it for him. And the boats were to bring stores and materials back to him on their return journeys.

But first he had to build a stable and a fenced yard for his horses, and a road from the land to the shore, a road that would cope with wagon loads of wood. And he had to build a jetty to which to moor the ketches. So they got to it and started cutting wood. This work proceeded slowly as at least twice a week they had to take the wagon fifteen miles to the tank at Murninnie for water – almost a full day's work in itself.

They lived on corned meat and damper with jam, for they had brought flour, jam and meat with them.

So it was quite some months before they were able to plant their first crops of turnips (for their leafy green tops) and potatoes.

Charlie lived an almost solitary life in his tent, with only his workmate, and a couple of neighbours who were some miles away. Occasionally one of the neighbours killed a cow or a sheep and sold him some fresh meat. And his sons fished from the ketches when they were held up by dodge tides.

So life got into a rhythm of cutting and carting wood and loading it onto the jetty, and loading the boats when they were in. Some chooks and turkeys were brought over, but the men seemed to spend a lot of time trying to catch them when they escaped. However, an egg or two made a nice change in the diet. Tinned meat, herrings, onions, sugar, baking powder and butter were also delivered by ketch from time to time. And every now and then his wife or daughters would bring his little children or grandchildren and stay in the tent for a week or two and cook for him, cake and roast mutton – once even a wayward turkey.

Charlie had a succession of workers to whom he sold stores, and kept accounts in the back of his diary so that he could deduct the cost from their wages when they moved on. Ten pounds of meat at fourpence ha'penny a pound, fifteen pounds of flour at tuppence a pound, sugar and onions were both threepence ha'penny a pound, a tin of herrings was sevenpence and a pound of tea sixpence. Occasionally some bacon or pork broke the monotony.

He never really made a go of growing crops; hay for the horses was the best he could manage. The ground was stony or sandy with very little soil and the rainfall intermittent. Charlie had been a mariner in his previous life so he kept track of the daily weather and the wind direction in his diary without fail. And also when the flies were bad.

One wonders how Charlie's stomach coped when he returned to civilisation for a Christmas break after three years on Eyre Peninsula.

The Tale of the Celery Growers

Driving home from the Mile End railway terminal with the window down and the wind blowing in your face, having just loaded a truck of delicious crunchy celery for the Victorian market, knowing the satisfaction of having brought the best celery in Australia to fruition from seed; and knowing that a fat cheque would arrive in the post in the following week – this surely was the best of times!

Trudging through the mud and sludge after a big storm, seeing all the half-grown seedlings washed down to the bottom of the hill, and knowing that you would have to start all over again; or suddenly noticing that the brown apple moth had visited in plague proportions boring their way up through the celery stalks leaving them inedible – indeed, these were the worst of times!

A plaque on a pedestal on the banks of the Torrens summarises the celery growers' story.

> Cyril John Emery bought the land when it was going dirt cheap during the Depression, but he died before he could get to farming it himself. Other members of the family had come into the Campbelltown area before this to grow vegetables and oranges. The fertile soil of the banks of the Torrens grew excellent produce of all sorts. Before the Millbrook reservoir was built during World War I, the river would periodically flood, covering the land with rich alluvial soil.

Edward Robert Emery (called Bob) was still a young man when he took up farming on Block 9 of Section 805 at Athelstone on the banks of the Torrens, just on the hills side of Schulze Road. On the property was an old brick and stone house where he and Nellie brought up six sons. Nellie always reckoned that the sound of white ants chomping away in the floorboards kept her awake at night, so the house was re-timbered. There was an old fireplace under the house suggesting that it had been built on the site of a pre-existing and original home, perhaps dating back to the 1850s when Pinkerton owned the property.

The six sons learnt the market gardener's trade by topping and tailing onions in the school holidays, but only two of them enjoyed the open air of the hot dry summers and the cold wet winters enough to take on the market garden. Cyril and Paul both started on the farm at the end of their schooling. Their father died when he was only fifty-one, leaving Nellie the task of running the market garden. Cyril and Paul were soon managing the place under the tutelage of Harry White, who had worked with their father.

From the outset, celery was the most successful crop. Cabbages, potatoes and onions filled in the season when the celery was finished. At first they grew tall green celery about four feet high, but then the stringless American variety Green Giant became popular; despite its name, it was only two feet high and much creamier in colour. The Emerys sold most of their celery to interstate markets first in Melbourne, then in Sydney.

Growing celery was successful in the Athelstone area. While the Bay of Biscay soil was fertile and retained moisture well, in winter it was sticky, slimy mud that stuck to the boys' boots and made it nigh impossible to walk. In summer, the clods that followed the plough would dry out and break down to a scarified consistency. The celery loved those conditions.

The soil was such that celery could be grown year after year, compared to other vegetables that could only be grown every second year. Water was easily come by too; a pump in the Torrens and a bore on the property provided good clean water. The bore water was said to have suddenly become saline after the 1954 earthquake; Athelstone sits on a fault line of the Adelaide geosyncline. At first, water was pumped into contoured furrows, but later, overhead sprinklers were used.

Growing celery was back-breaking work. In transplanting seedlings into four-inch-deep furrows, the gardener had to stand on the edge of the furrow, lean over, make a hole with his dibber, push the plant into the hole and then compact the soil around it, again with his dibber. Up, down, up, down, all day long. Backaches in the middle of the night!

Before cutting the mature product, the double rows of plants had to be boarded up with sheets of galvanised iron or the sides of packing crates to keep the stalks upright and pale in colour. Before the cut celery could be sent to the market, water was hosed onto the stalks to clean them and then the celery trimmed to size to fit the packing cases.

Growing celery was a seven-day-a-week job. Cyril and Paul could only have alternate Sundays off. A tight daily schedule of planting successive batches of seedlings all through the early summer to the early autumn months, followed by boarding and cutting beginning before the last seedlings were even planted, kept them at it from daylight till dark each day. Celery took just over three months to grow in the warmer weather and up to five months when it got colder.

At times, growing celery could be a heart-breaking venture. Immunity of pests and diseases to sprays and the never-ending catalogue of new diseases had to be vigilantly watched for and battled against. The fungus fire blight would attack when it was warm and wet, and the celery had to be sprayed weekly to prevent the leaves going brown. Salinity in the bore water also had to be watched, for too much salt affected the plants.

The coming of the Ferguson tractor in the late 1940s transformed the gardening process, but it put the horse out of a job. The horse was called Smithy because on his first day at the garden Charles Kingsford Smith flew over the property on his way home from a trip to Melbourne. Smithy was occasionally called out of retirement to pull a specially made sledge to cart the celery out when conditions got too boggy for the tractor and trailer. Smithy hated being hit on the rump; his instinctive reaction was to kick out. No wonder he was bought cheaply. Being a slightly lazy worker, he lived to a good old age.

The advent of supermarkets changed the fiscal state of affairs for all vegetable growers. Whereas the market gardener had named his price in the wholesale market, the supermarket looked for the buyer with the lowest prices. So everyone was forced to cut their prices. Sometimes they would hardly cover costs and a decent wage. And if the supermarket decided to have a big celery promotion, they would pay even less to the growers. It was a lose–lose situation.

So the Emerys continued to send their celery interstate by train or refrigerated truck. The trick was to cut it at just the right time so that it would arrive in Melbourne overnight or in Sydney after a two-day journey, as crisp and fresh as it was when it left the garden. Sydney trains needed ice packed in them to help with the process: packed in the carriage, not in the boxes of celery. The Emerys reckoned that while their celery might occasionally fall a teeny bit short of being the best, it was always known as the best traveller.

In the early nineties, the family sold the land for residential development. Cyril and Paul relocated their market gardening to Virginia. Now retired, and when not watching the cricket on the telly, Paul sometimes goes for walks with his wife along Linear Park, rests a while on the seat near the family plaque on the banks of the Torrens and ponders his celery growing days, both the best of times and the worst of times.

Historical Stories

While all of these stories are based on historical information, they are in fact fictional.

Leonardo and the Crab

The year 2002 was an occasion for celebrating the second centenary of Matthew Flinders' 1802 voyage of discovery and circumnavigation of Australia. The SA Art Gallery commemorated the occasion with an exhibition of paintings and drawings executed by the naturalists from both the *Investigator* and the *Geographe*. Among these was the original paint-by-numbers sketch of a blue swimmer crab, along with the finished product.

My christening in 1760 was a low-key affair. Being the fifth child of an ailing court painter whose income was dwindling along with his life, I didn't have the full fanfare as the water was poured, just a blessing.

Next year found us children in an orphanage as our father had left this earth, and mother in her grief couldn't cope. We all liked to doodle with pencils and paint when given the chance, be it on paper, pavement or walls.

The parish priest, who liked small boys, noticed the talent of us brothers, and set us to drawing all the plants and flowers in the orphanage garden. He even gifted us with pencils and colours to carry out the task. No doubt he was going to make a pretty penny from them in the marketplace later.

When I left the orphanage due to my advancing years, I moved to Vienna and got a job illustrating Count Niklaus's tome on rare plants. Such was the quality of my work that they nicknamed me Leonardo. Then a visiting Oxford professor engaged me to travel the Mediterranean with him painting flora and fauna, from vast vistas of sea shores to thousands of minuscule shells on the waterline.

The professor took me back to England with him and found me a position for the princely sum of £315 per annum on the research ship the *Investigator*, working with the naturalist Robert Brown under the command of Captain Matthew Flinders. Off to the Great South Land we sailed, and all around it too. A rough passage we had of it getting there. I spent much time in my hammock with a pail nearby, but eventually I got used to the swell and the dip of the monstrous seas.

I could get lost in the reverie of accurately illustrating plants and animals for Mr Brown, for I liked to record them perfectly, right down to the glint in the beady eye of a living creature, or the fine filaments of eucalyptus blossoms.

'Ah, Leonardo,' crooned Captain Flinders when he came to see how things were progressing. 'A fine artist thou art, Ferdinand Bauer, and a prodigious one too, so Brown tells me. Keep up the good work.' And as a second thought he added, 'Perhaps you could draw me a lovely creature to grace my parlour wall when I get home.'

High praise indeed, falling like nectar of the gods and inebriating my soul with gratification. At first I thought he might appreciate the likeness of a black-collared parrot that I had painted near Boston Bay, using nigh on two hundred separate hues of verdure for his magnificent plumage. Then I wondered whether he might prefer my weedy sea dragon with its delicate appendages of vermilion and ochre.

A few days later we happened to be on a sandy shore way up in Spencers Gulf beneath the lee of the mountain Flinders named after Mr Brown. Here I caught a crab, or rather the crab caught me. Mr Brown told me that it was a blue swimmer crab. Did you ever see such a beautiful creature? I called him Bluey. It was just before sunset when we were to set sail again, for the waters were very shallow in these parts. Not time enough to complete a finished portrait, so I just pencilled the crab onto my sheet of paper, delineating all the areas of different colours by a system of numbers. Both sides of him, top and under.

When we got back to England many months later, I painstakingly coloured every little detail of my crab, blending hues of azure and marine with ivory and titanium white and touches of sienna and burnt umber. A thing of beauty it turned out to be. Good enough for publishing. But you can do a job too well. The effort required to engrave and colour the details of my illustrations was beyond the scope of any publisher and only ten plates appeared in Flinders' journals. How disappointing when I had completed over two thousand exquisite drawings. So I parcelled up

the crab picture and sent it to Captain Flinders, and packed up most of
the rest of my precious paintings and took them back to Austria with me
and hung them on my own walls.

A Policeman's Lot...

The outline of this journey to Innamincka of Constable John Finn
was detailed in the (Police) Station Journals of Innamincka in 1934. I
came across it when researching family history in the Station Journals
at State Records of SA. Ten years later, my father was the policeman at
Innamincka, so I wondered whether he had had similar troubles in his
policing of the district.

I'd been away in Adelaide on annual leave for 1934 and was travelling
back to my station in the outback. It had been fine and hot in Adelaide,
perfect swimming weather. My old Ford T was really a bit of a bomb by
now but it was all I had and all I could afford on my meagre pay packet,
for we police had to provide our own means of transport. When I got to
Broken Hill, I phoned the inspector to let him know that my leave was
finished and as of tomorrow, 18 February, I was officially on duty again.

Next day, I set out northwards to Innamincka, covering a good seventy-
five miles on this first day, camping in the creek at Fowlers Gap to escape
the ever-present spinifex and gibbers, for spinifex, gibbers and bedrolls
don't mix for a good night's sleep. No chance of rain coming to wash me
down the creek – it was the middle of a dry and hot, hot summer.

On the Monday, the travelling was good too, except for the flies, until
I was about ten miles south of Milparinka, where I could see thunder
clouds on the flat horizon. All the creeks began to run – there must have
been rain upstream – at first just a dribble, then a rapid flow. Branches
and twigs, the odd snake and dead kangaroo, and all sorts of rubbish were
carried along the surface, probably from far away. But still I pushed on,
which in retrospect was a stupid thing to do, for it wasn't long before I
was in the midst of heavy thunderstorms and continuous lightning.

Just south of Tibooburra, my little car got caught in a flooded creek.
The water seeped right through the floorboards. I was afraid of being

washed down the creek, even drowned perhaps. So I abandoned the car on the nearest bank, walked the three miles into Tibooburra and got a bloke with a truck and a winch to come and haul the car out. Then the Ford and I staggered into town like a drunk and disorderly with the hiccups. I spent another night in my swag under one of the pile of great granite boulders on the edge of Tibooburra – no sky full of bright stars to light up the night.

For the next three days, it rained and rained, and then it rained some more. It literally poured down. The whole country was awash. Loud was the noise of the water swishing and swirling down the creek. No, it wasn't a creek any more, but a raging torrent.

Eventually a further three days later, the rain eased and finally stopped and the searing sun came out again, but I still had to wait for the bloody country to dry out and the creeks to reduce their flow. What else could I do in a one-horse town like Tibooburra but sit in the pub imbibing a few and playing cards with some other stranded travellers? At least I could ensure that the pub was closed at six o'clock.

Two days later, the southward-bound mail truck went by, five days late, so I presumed that it might be OK to proceed. I set out again, being now more than a week overdue.

The car coped until I was about twelve miles north of Naryilco Station, when she developed ignition trouble and the condenser cut out. It was a long way to walk back over the gibber – and the sharp little stones caused havoc to the soles of my boots – to Naryilco to get another one, but it had to be done.

Quite adept at fixing cars after several years in the bush, I fitted the condenser myself then camped for the night. But all was not well,. The old Ford was past it. I only managed a further fifty miles, reaching Timbanacka Swamp, when there was a huge bang, the engine stopped and we came to a shuddering halt. Getting under the car, I found that the battery box had collapsed; the battery had fallen out and was smashed to pieces. Damn and blast it all! Left her to the mosquitoes under a coolibah tree at Timbanacka Swamp until sometime in the future when I could get someone to drag her back into civilisation and fix her.

Now I had to sit by the side of the road and wait for the mail truck to return in order to get to Innamincka, for there wasn't any other traffic on the track. It was due on Friday, still three bloody days away. Good thing I always take a book along with me for just such occasions.

So eventually I got my ride to Nappa Merrie just east of the SA–Queensland border, then after another day of travelling west, the mail truck delivered me home again. At least the mail truck could manage the huge red sandhills on this part of the track. So a fortnight after my leave had finished, I got back to the station at Innamincka and made friends again with Police Horse Joker.

Archer

Archer won the first Melbourne Cup in 1861.

You know, it's all a big fat furphy that I walked from Sydney to Melbourne for the first Cup race. No self-respecting horse would walk that far then expect to be fresh enough to run a two-mile race. Mind you I often walked thirty or forty miles to run races in nearby towns, but seven hundred miles, give it a go! Some fancy journalist thought that such a long walk would make a good story and so it entered the halls of fable.

I travelled by boat, a steamer from Nowra to Sydney, then from Sydney to Melbourne with only a day or two before the big race to get over the seasickness and be able to stand steady on four legs again after the pounding and swelling motion of the waves.

I was by that time a six-year-old stallion, a fine piece of horse (even if I do say so myself), standing at sixteen hands with powerful hindquarters, a deep girth, well-sprung ribs and a good head and neck. Nicknamed the Bull, I was, and proud of it. I always hung my tongue out of my mouth when I raced. And with my long strides and unusual rolling galloping gait, what better signs of a stand-out hero horse!

Anyway, back to that first race at Flemington. It was the first Thursday of November of 1861, a wet day that muddied and slowed the track. Seventeen of us lined up for the start. I wasn't really a sure bet – I'd been slightly injured in training a few days beforehand – but my trainer, Etienne de Mestre, placed a large bet on his favourite horse, me, not my stablemates Exeter and Inheritor.

I got away to a bad start, then three horses fell and there was mayhem. Two of them died in the fall, the other bolted away across the course, leaving his jockey in agony on the ground. It slowed the whole field down trying to avoid getting caught up in the mêlée. It wasn't until the last turn that I finally got my act together and outran Mormon to win the race.

So I became famous for being the first winner of the Melbourne Cup, in the fastest time. Naturally it was the fastest time as it was the first of the now famous race. But it went down in history as being the slowest time on record. Three minutes, fifty-two seconds it took. Who cares about time? I won, didn't I? That's all that matters, and Mr Etienne has the gold watch and a bag of gold sovereigns to prove it. On the very next day, I won another two-mile race, the Melbourne Town Plate, in the same time.

In the following year, I went to Flemington again. This time we left much earlier, giving us a chance to recover from the journey. In preparation, Exeter and I were walked to Geelong to banish the collywobbles from the sea journey. I started as favourite in 1862 and didn't disappoint. So I became the first favourite to win the Cup, as well as the first non-favourite. My time that year was five seconds faster than the previous year.

I was looking forward to winning a third time, but didn't get the chance because Etienne dilly-dallied about whether I was up to going or not, and my acceptance arrived too late, due to it being a public holiday in Melbourne, so no one was at work to receive my application on its due date. In sympathy, other interstate horses boycotted the race, so there were only seven starters, all from Victoria.

After more injuries that prevented me from racing at all, I went back to Jembaicumbene and stood stud, siring several foals, but none of them could match their sire in victory. With hairs from my elegant tail, some woman made a horseshoe-shaped ornament that has lived in the Australian Racing Museum in Melbourne ever since. So you could go and stroke my famous hair if you like. It might bring you some luck.

Ah Ping's Gold

Ah Ping's Gold was written to accompany the history component of the National Australian Curriculum for primary schools.

I'm Ah Ping and I'm twelve years old. I live on a farm in China with my parents, two older brothers, three younger sisters and one set of grandparents.

I don't speak English. I asked my great uncle, who is a scribe in both Chinese and English, to translate this for me so that you could read it.

March 1854: Kwang-Chou province near Hong Kong in China

The elders of my family have decided to go to the Land of the New Gold Mountain, to go to New South Wales, where we hear there is gold at Ophir. They decided that the men of the family would go, that the women and my oldest brother would stay home to look after the farm. We have been getting poorer and poorer here as the land has been divided between so many young men in our family. My father had to borrow money to pay for our fares. He will have to pay it back with gold sent home from the diggings. We are hoping to find plenty of gold.

My father, my older brother, three uncles, grandfather, great-uncle and me, all would go. My grandfather and his brother were not old men, but respected as elders. We all have the family name Ah. My brother is Ah Chong, my father is Ah Lim and my grandfather is Ah Lu.

June 1854: Port Jackson in New South Wales

Several family groups came together to set out as one large group. Among us were a herbalist, a scribe and a barber to shave the men's faces. We came in a three-masted ship with sails flying in the breeze. It was smelly, dirty and cramped. Sometimes it was so rough that we felt seasick and had to stay below in our tightly squeezed little bunks where we slept. Actually, I thought it was better to stay on deck when feeling sick, just in case. It was easier to clean up on the deck.

Sometimes we saw sleek porpoises diving in and out of the water.

After three months we landed in Port Jackson, which is quite a big town.

In Port Jackson, the men bought all the necessary things: tents, picks and shovels, sieves and buckets, cooking pots and rice, and vegetable seeds.

We then set out on the long journey by foot carrying all our things in bundles tied to long poles balanced on our shoulders. We wore cone-shaped hats, rope sandals, long tunics and loose pants. We walked a hundred and fifty miles on the tracks over the Blue Mountains.

Lots of people passed us on the way. Everyone seemed to be heading for the gold fields. Some shouted at us, 'Go home, Chink.'

Although we couldn't understand the words, we understood the message perfectly. I was scared they might attack us but felt safe with all the adults.

August 1854: Sofala at Ophir

The tracks were horrible – wet, muddy and slippery, steep and rocky. Progress was slow and our feet were very sore. At night we camped around a fire to dry out and have a meal of rice. It took three weeks to get here. It seemed like ages.

But here we are, on the banks of the Turon River. We put up our tents on the edge of the camping area. Everyone had tents or a piece of canvas thrown over a branch, with a fire at the opening. Snakes and insects often visited our tents at night. Thank goodness, no snakes bit us, but insects surely did. There was a hotel and a shop and only a couple of other wooden buildings.

The trooper came to collect our mining licence fee of thirty shillings. There seemed to be thousands of people, many Chinese.

The Australians look and sound strange and different to us. They have bushy hair, wear leather around their waists, and eat damper and mutton. They shout a lot and sing rowdy songs at night. And they smell of perspiration and grog.

One of the first things our men did was to build a joss house, a house of prayer, out of wood and bark. We decorated it and then burnt incense in it before a little statue of the God of Hope. The incense and some offerings were to thank our ancestors for a safe journey and to pray for good luck.

December 1854: Sofala

We've been here for three months now. Our people work as a team. My grandfather is in charge of our group. We met other groups of Chinese here too.

Sometimes we pan for gold. We put river gravel in the pan with some water and swirl it around. This washes away the dirt and stones and leaves the gold behind because it is heavier.

Sometimes we puddle for gold. The dirt and clay is put in a large tub with some water and stirred up. When the tub is emptied some gold might be at the bottom.

The Australians sometimes cradle for gold. Gravel is put into the top of a wooden cradle. The cradle is rocked while water is poured through it. Gold can be caught at the bottom.

Gold that is got in any of those ways is called alluvial gold. It is found on the bed of the river. Often it is only in very small specks.

The Australians sometimes dig shafts like a well, and make tunnels under the ground to find reef gold in the rocks. We don't like to do that in case we upset the gods of the earth. We prefer to pick over what others have already left.

Some of our people are making a garden of vegetables that we hope to eat, and to have enough to sell. Some are cooking food and selling it to the many men who are here without their wives. Some are using the cooking pots to wash clothes in for Australian people as well as ourselves. The barber is doing a roaring trade with Australians as well as Chinese. So we get money in other ways as well as finding gold.

You would think with all these services we provide for the other miners that they would appreciate us, but they are very unfriendly and call us names. They can't understand us and grizzle that we work hard seven days a week while they take a day off for drinking lots of beer, singing loudly and kicking a funny-shaped ball. Sometimes even the adults worry about our safety.

January 1855: Sofala

January is hot and dusty. The creek is nearly dried up, and the ground is much harder to work. We are having to put the used washing water on our gardens.

Some of our men have found good amounts of gold. We send most of it home by post to our families. We could take it to the agent who would weigh it and give us money for it. That's what Australians do, but what would our families do with Australian money?

Native people come to our tents sometimes, as they live just beyond the edge of the camp in shelters made of bushes. A group of them came with several fish the other day. In return, we gave them some carrots and potatoes but, although we couldn't understand them, we could see that they didn't know what to do with them, so we showed them. There's few things as tasty as a freshly washed carrot eaten raw. And we buried a potato in the coals of our fire to show them how to cook the potatoes.

There were a couple of boys with them who beckoned to me and my brother to follow them. They took us to a waterhole, where we took off our clothes like them and jumped in. So cool and refreshing, and good to get the whole body wet instead of just washing in a bucket. One of them gently pulled my pigtail and held it up to have a good look. So I traced my fingers across the scars on his chest. It was a pity that we couldn't tell each other the why and how of our differences.

Then they showed us how to catch yabbies. We took some home; they were good with rice and vegetables. Our father wasn't really happy with us going off like that, but...

17 February 1855: Sofala

Today it is the Chinese New Year, a big day of celebration for us. 1855 is the Year of the Rabbit. We didn't have our usual firecrackers, so we built a big bonfire and danced around it. And afterwards Ah Chong and I played mah-jong with ivory tiles and dice. I made the most matching sets of tiles, so I won. The older men just sat smoking their opium. My father and his friend practised some kung fu.

Late February 1855: Sofala

It's even hotter than last month, if possible. Last night there was a thunderstorm with some rain that cooled things down a bit.

Last week when I was helping with the panning, I came upon a nugget of gold the size of my thumb. I put it in my pocket quickly without telling anyone about it. I wanted this one for myself. But later on I started worrying about it. Where would I hide it so that no one else could find it? I didn't want anyone discovering my hiding place, so it had to be in our own camp, not in a hole high in a tree like I first thought. If I buried it, someone would be sure to wonder why digging had been going on in that spot. I decided to sew it into the waistline of my pants. It wouldn't be noticed there, as my top always hung down to my knees.

The natives came again, this time with a kangaroo that they cut up and asked us for money for. They sold some to a few Australians too. They hung about for a while so the men made them some tea to drink. I took the boy that looked about my age off into the bushes and showed him my nugget.

'Come,' he indicated. This time he took me up a hill and showed me some rocks with bits that glistened like my nugget. 'Same,' he said.

We both scratched away and managed to dislodge a chunk about the size of an egg. He didn't want it. I don't think he even knew that it was valuable, and that it was what all the fuss was about around here.

This one was too big to hide so I took it back to the camp to my grandfather, who was excited, very excited indeed. So early next morning just as it was beginning to get light I showed him where it had come from. He brought his pick with him. He managed to dig out another egg-sized lump.

'We'll keep quiet about this,' he said. 'We don't want anyone else to know that we're out here.'

We were back again as the sun broke through the pink clouds over the mountains to the east. It took two weeks of secret morning excursions by different members of our family before the gold was all gone from that rock.

March 1855: Sofala

I am still worried about my own little nugget, and the trouble I will be in if my father knew about it. I decided to put it behind the God of Hope on the shelf in the joss house. No one would be looking behind there, and I could keep the place dusted.

1 April 1855: Sofala

It was a Sunday, and lots of Australians were gathered near the pub. They were shouting and waving banners with 'No Chinese wanted here' written on them. Some of them had spades in their hands, but they don't work on Sundays. They were looking over towards our camp, fiercely. I was worried.

My father came running over to me and my brother and said, 'Quick, hide. I fear we're in trouble.'

We found an empty shaft to squat in but we could clearly hear what was going on. People rushed towards our camp, shouting at us. Our men stood ready in a line to halt them, but they were just pushed over.

The angry Australians ran straight through our men, knocked over our tent and kicked our cooking pots and panning gear out of the way. 'Where's your opium?' they shouted. 'Give us your opium. Give us your gold. This place belongs to us not to you. Get out.'

Others shouted, 'April fools. Go home, you April fools.' One of them ran to the joss house with a branch of dead leaves. He pushed over my grandfather, who was trying to guard it. It was a special place for us where we worshipped our ancestors and the God of Hope. Someone set fire to it. We smelt the smoke as it billowed into the air and heard the cracking of burning wood.

My gold nugget, I thought, what will happen to it? But right now wasn't the time for thinking about that. I could hear my grandfather moaning. He must have been hurt. So I crept out to find out how he was.

The people had gone by now. We heard the troopers firing their pistols telling them to leave us alone and go back to their own camps.

I found my grandfather writhing on the ground. He had fallen onto a sharp rock and gashed his head. There was lots of blood. It looked bad.

'Quick, get father and the herbalist,' I shouted at Ah Chong. 'Grandfather is hurt!'

I cradled my grandfather's head in my arms while I waited. Just as they arrived, he took a long deep breath and died. It was so sad. He had been our leader and he loved us all a lot.

2 April 1855: Sofala

Today we buried my grandfather up the hill, near to the God of the Mountains. His brother, the scribe, chiselled out his name on a piece of flat rock that we used for a headstone. We prayed that the God of Hope would be good to him in his next life.

7 April 1855: Sofala

My father decided that he and his two boys would go back to China to share the news with the women of the family. It would be sad meeting again.

When I was packing my things into a bundle, I remembered my little nugget. I went to where the joss house had stood and sifted through the ashes. After a while, I found it stuck to a piece of timber. It had melted and was now flat like a misshapen coin. It came off the wood quite easily, so I slipped it back into my waistband. I decided that I would give it to my grandmother as a remembrance of her husband. Then I wouldn't have to feel guilty about it any more. Our native friends gave us a possum skin rug to take home to my grandmother.

Ghosts At Mamray Park

This story was awarded second place in the Mature Writer section of the City of Campbelltown Literary Competition in 2012. It was written to the theme of 'Taking care of business' and inspired by the image of a ghost on the balcony of Murray Park House on the Links wall hanging in the foyer of the City of Campbelltown Library and its explanation on the website Links_Wallhanging_Booklet on www.campbelltown.sa.gov.au

Kirsty Douvakis, a student of social science, was researching the history of the university's heritage-listed main building. She went to inspect the fifteen-roomed house and noted its solid bluestone walls, its imposing tower, rendered quoins and hipped and gabled roof. She photographed the front, side and back views, the balcony, balustrade and bay window, and took close-ups of the delicate cast-iron lacework decorating the front veranda.

That night, as she viewed the day's work on her computer, she noticed on a photograph of the grand staircase in the entrance hall a faint image of a young child swinging on the banister at the foot of the stairs. She looked as if she was pining to go with the person leaving by the front door.

That's funny, she thought, there was no one around when I took that shot. She enlarged the printout which, while it was largely pixellated, did show more detail. She noticed the fair curly hair, big brown eyes and tiny ballerina slippers.

Excitedly she showed her boyfriend, Dazza, who screeched, 'Oh my God, how out of this world! Is she a ghost or something?' Stopping for breath he then continued, 'Take another look. She's a bit like you, especially round the forehead and eyes.'

Kirsty agreed. 'I had hair like that at that age. But doesn't she look so miserable?'

Who was this child? A resident of the big house or a visitor sleeping overnight or perhaps a niece staying for a holiday?

Next week, Kirsty went to the local history section of the nearby library to research the building. Information about the house and the family who had owned it was plentiful. Judge Benjamin Brooks lived there with his single sister, Elizabeth. He needed a big house to entertain his numerous guests. Built by his parents in about 1885, it was extended in 1910 so that Benjamin could accommodate visitors from the country.

'You can see the house on our Links wall hanging,' said the librarian, who took her to the foyer to inspect the exquisitely detailed and beautiful work.

When they finally located the appropriate cameo on the vast quilt, Kirsty noticed a shadowy figure of a woman staring out of an upper bay window of Mamray Park House.

The librarian told her, 'Some claim to have seen the ghost of a woman pacing up and down along the balustrade above that bay window. As if she was looking longingly and waiting for someone to come back.'

While she was there, Kirsty showed the librarian her photo of the child.

'Mmm, I think I've heard of that happening to other photographers too,' said the librarian. 'I would be almost certain that we have a picture of that child.' She rummaged through her filing cabinet drawer and found a formal photo of the same little girl. 'See,' she said, turning over the photo to reveal some neat calligraphy on its reverse, 'her name was Eleanor Armand. That seems to be a French name. She was five when this was taken in 1921. I wonder what she was doing in the house.'

Kirsty was consumed with curiosity about the mysterious child. So she searched the Births, Deaths and Marriages records for a birth of Eleanor Armand in about 1916, and found that her mother was Annie Armand.

I bet she was a looker to have a beautiful child like that. A real French beauty, curvy and seductive, she thought. I wonder who she married? Then she looked for a marriage over a ten-year period of an Annie to a Mr Armand, but no success. So on the off-chance, she tried for a marriage of Annie Armand as her maiden name. She was very surprised to find that she had married Alfred Stephenson in 1914, a couple of years before her daughter's birth. Why did she register Eleanor's surname as Armand and not that of her husband, Stephenson?

Kirsty and Dazza pondered the matter further, speculating about all sorts of reasons for the situation. Perhaps Alf wasn't her father after all. War service records on the internet revealed that Alf Stephenson went to Gallipoli in 1915, too early to be Eleanor's father. He returned in 1919, gassed and depressed, and no doubt moody and unpredictable. Obviously not the man Annie had fallen in love with five years previously.

'Let's try the death records,' said Dazza, 'and check out when Alf died.'

This they did.

'Look,' exclaimed Dazza, peering over her shoulder. 'It says that he died by his own hand at the Yatala Labour Prison in 1921. That's about as depressed as you can get. What on earth was he doing in prison?'

'Court records next,' whooped Kirsty. This entailed a trip to State Records in the city, where they found that Alf had been sentenced by Judge Benjamin Brooks. Was this a coincidence? they thought.

Time to discover more about Judge Benjamin Brooks. Kirsty googled him and he came up on the *Australian Dictionary of Biography* database, complete with a photograph. She was intrigued at the similarity in appearance of Eleanor Armand to Benjamin. Same tall skinny frame, same mouth and chin, along with dusty fair hair.

'Perhaps Benjamin was her father,' queried Kirsty, 'despite the fact that he was an upright man, unmarried and a pillar of the community?'

Dazza chimed in, 'Did he seduce the beautiful Annie, if only the once? Perhaps Eleanor and her mother lived at Mamray House.'

'Yes, that could be it,' said Kirsty. 'Annie could have been a maid.'

So they tracked back to the local library to see if any house records still existed. They did. Annie was a domestic in the house from 1915, just after Alf had left for the war, until 1921, just after Alf had died. Was Annie the ghostly woman on the balustrade? What drove her to such lengths? Was she pining for Alf and lost love?

Kirsty remembered Alf's crime from the court material that she had brought home. Aggravated assault against Judge Benjamin Brooks. In 1919 soon after arriving home from the war, he was arrested in the city outside the judge's chambers with gun in hand and shouting, 'You bastard! Taking advantage of a woman while her man is away fighting for the motherland. I'll get you for this!'

Kirsty was sure that Alf had just come home from war and found that Annie had a daughter that couldn't possibly be his, given the time frame. He had put two and two together, and in a blinding rage had decided to do something about it. A newspaper report at the time revealed that he was sentenced for twenty years and the charge had been upgraded to attempted murder.

'Poor Annie, how did she cope with all this?' Kirsty was feeling for her. 'Bad enough that Alf went away to war and came back only half the man. And then sent to prison seemingly forever, where after a very short while he took his own life. No wonder she stalked the balcony at night. No wonder Eleanor was looking to leave the house with anyone who would give her some loving attention.'

When next she had a chance, Kirsty went back to her home in the country and told her mother of these exciting discoveries. She showed Marj the picture of Eleanor.

Her mother went a deathly white and had to sit down for a minute. 'Oh, my gosh, that child could easily be my own grandmother. But her name was Ellie Almond. Hang on a minute while I find the photo.'

It was almost certainly the same child, the same ringlets, a similar style simple white dress, and an exact match for the slipper-shoes.

Excitedly Marj exclaimed, 'Of course, Ellie must have been christened Eleanor, and we must have got the spelling of the surname wrong down through the years.'

Kirsty suggested that they check their ancestry on the Births, Deaths and Marriages records again. Sure enough, the surname wasn't Almond but Armand. So Ellie was Kirsty's great grandmother and Annie was her great great grandmother.

And the judge was her great great grandfather.

Marj and Kirsty laughed, realising that in sentencing Alf, Judge Brooks was just taking care of the whole goddamn awful business.

The New Year Picnic Train

1 January 2015 was the hundredth anniversary of the incident that this fictional story is based on.

'Mummy, I'm so excited,' exclaimed twelve-year-old Mabel. 'The New Year Picnic will be so special, I just know it.'

'Sure will,' replied Rose, her mother. 'Put on your hat, dear. It's going to be a scorcher today.'

'Come along, hurry up.' George was impatient. 'We don't want to miss the train.'

Each year the local business Manchester Unity put on a picnic at Silverton for the Broken Hill members of their Order of Oddfellows. In 1915, more than a thousand people happily gathered at the train station waiting to be ushered into open ore-wagons that had been hosed out for the short journey.

'A hundred per wagon,' yelled the mayor, who was controlling the loading of people.

Other men bustled about importantly carrying boxes of chops and sausages and bottles of tomato sauce and fizzy drinks for the chop picnic and packing them into a covered railway carriage.

With a great gush of steam and a loud whistle blast, the train slowly pulled out of the station.

'Hooray,' yelled the excited passengers. 'We're off at last!' Many shouted and waved to their neighbours in adjacent wagons.

With the wind streaming past them, both ladies and gentlemen had to hang onto their hats lest they be blown away.

'What fun!' cried Mabel to her friend Izzy, whose family had ended up in the same wagon.

They had barely even settled down when ten minutes later an explosion rang out from the embankment at the side of the train.

'Oooh, fireworks, that's new this year,' cried Rose.

'And I saw Mr Goolie's ice-cream cart over there too. Perhaps we'll all get a free ice cream.' Mabel was hopeful. 'See their turbans and a flag draped over the side of the cart. How pretty is that?'

But excitement turned to fear as more shots rang out. One caught Izzy in the head, and she fell to the floor, blood running all over her new muslin dress. Adults rushed to her aid, but it wasn't long before she breathed her last. Her mother was distraught, cradling her child's head and moaning loudly. Mabel screamed.

Several others along the train also received gunshot wounds. The train slowed to a halt.

'What the hell?' yelled George. 'What's going on?' He recognised the red flag with its white star and crescent moon as that of the Ottoman Empire. He had read in the *Barrier Miner* last week that the Ottoman Empire had joined Germany against the British Empire and her allies in the Great War. He was sorely afraid of what could transpire. He remembered a lone individual shooting at Archduke Ferdinand of Austria had started the Great War in Europe. And here were two lone Afghanis attacking a whole train full of people in outback Australia. But why?

Goolie had come to the outback from northern India near the border with Afghanistan a number of years ago as a camel team driver. Sick of walking with his camel load of goods across the waterless interior of the Australian continent, he had settled on the western periphery of Broken Hill at Ghantown, where a number of other cameleers lived. He had swapped his camels for an ice cream cart, and walking the desert for walking the streets of Broken Hill tempting small children who talked their mothers into the purchase of a cone full of deliciously cold ice cream. But while the children always welcomed him with glee, their parents weren't so friendly. With clauses of the White Australia policy ringing in their ears, not to mention the sound of the mullah calling Muslims to worship several times a day, they were always wary and not the least bit friendly.

Goolie's friend, the mullah Abdul, had set up a business in the lean-to shed in his backyard butchering meat halal style for the many Muslims who lived in the town. But he had run foul of the sanitary inspector, who tried to close him down as he didn't hold the requisite license for killing animals. Seething with rage at the situation and the many taunts about their origins and religion, Abdul had complained long and loud to Goolie, threatening revenge on 'them whites'. Goolie, who was extremely patriotic and had previously fought for the Turkish army in four campaigns, sympathised deeply with his mullah. The New Year Picnic train gathered a huge number of 'them whites' in one place where they were unable to counter-attack or escape. The perfect situation.

Together they took their weapons in the ice cream cart along with the flag of the Ottoman Empire, and set themselves up on the embankment beside the train line about three miles out of town, waiting with their rifles until the train came by.

With great whoops of glee, they fired off several rounds with uncanny accuracy, killing three people and wounding several others. Then the enormity of what they had done hit them, so they fled on foot with their guns and took shelter in the rocky outcrops of Cable Hill.

Stan Milligan, police chief in Broken Hill, received a message about the train hold-up, and hastily called up the resident militia along with anyone else who cared to join them, donned his pith helmet and rode out at full speed to the train, collecting Jimmy the Aboriginal tracker on the way.

Jimmy picked up the trail and led them to Cable Hill, where a shoot-out ensued. Abdul received a direct hit in the chest which finished him off, while Goolie was taken to hospital to be treated for his wounds, but he died soon after arriving. Constable Harris was also shot and wounded in the mêlée.

At his nagging wife's insistence, Jim Raftery was down at his wood heap cutting wood for the stove, despite the desperate heat of the day. His two-roomed stone cottage, a hovel really, was half a mile away from Cable Hill. With perspiration dripping from his forehead and neck, he was suddenly hit by a stray bullet from the battle and knocked over. His wife, investigating the sudden cessation in chopping sounds, found him dead, sprawled on the mallee stumps.

While retracing his steps three days later, Stan Milligan found a note stashed in a crevice between two rocks at Cable Hill. Written by Goolie, it proclaimed, 'I will fight and kill your people because your people are fighting my country.' Abdul had added his own comment: 'Allah Akbar, God is great.'

Mabel read the story in the paper several days later. Perplexed, she asked her mother, 'But God is great, isn't he?'

Inspired By Antiques Roadshow

The following were inspired by stories on the television series *Antiques Roadshow*, or by articles in British magazines.

Glengyle House

1997, a year to remember, the year we bought the place for a song! Well, not really for a song. It was actually extremely expensive, but small in price when compared to what we hoped to make from it. The old lady wasn't very happy, though; her children hadn't consulted her about selling it and it was, after all, still her home.

We planned to keep the essence of the grand old house while building luxury retirement units on the extensive old garden. We hoped to retain many of the old palm trees and ancient gums. The antiquated kitchen on the back would have to go. We could add something more substantial in its place, as long as we kept within Heritage guidelines. A new door would have to be installed in the back wall, but that was the only alteration needed to the house itself.

Situated on Lower North East Road, Glengyle House was indeed one of great beauty and simplicity. Two-storeyed, built of river stone and with a couple of chimneys, its elegant return verandas on front and sides, complete with delicate wrought-iron lacework and balustrades, added a sense of genteel refinement to the overall picture. While no upkeep had been done for many years, it promised to be relatively easy to restore to its former glory with a coat of plaster and a lick of paint.

The previous owners had been generous enough to leave behind some authentic period furniture. I could just imagine the drawing room in a new deep salmon colour with the ornate ceiling rose, and woodwork of white bordering a pale carpet. The carved wood and brick, mirrored fireplace would have to stay, but no more smoky fires in it, though!

Today we finished demolishing the old kitchen attached to the back of the house. The most delicate part of the work was taking out the door in order to replace it with a larger one. Carefully we removed the cracked lintel above the doorway when, bugger me, out dropped a pair of very worn child's boots and a brown paper bag of some sort of seeds. The leather ankle-high boots with their studded lacing holes were as stiff as a corpse by now. And the seeds were black and shrivelled – they looked a bit like sunflower seeds. What on earth were they doing up there all of that time? The place must be more than a hundred years old by now.

I took the boots and seeds home to my wife, who has a passion for old things, to see what she would make of them.

'I saw something like this on *Antiques Roadshow* once,' she said. 'Apparently it was fairly common back in the early nineteenth century to leave a pair of old boots and some seeds in the wall space above the lintel. Be blowed if I can remember what the significance was, though – good luck or something. Leave it with me. I'll google it.'

*

After a long and traumatic journey halfway across the world, Joseph Linden, his wife Lizzie and two children arrived at Port Misery on the *Lady Emma* in the unaccustomed heat of December 1837. They soon settled into a small cottage in Hindley Street in Adelaide and set to growing watermelons and vegetables on the banks of the Torrens down from the house. Surplus fruit and vegetables were sold on Joseph's greengrocery stall, along with a sideline in seeds.

But Joseph wanted more. He wanted some fertile land and a spacious house in which his family could grow and prosper. Setting out east along the River Torrens, he had walked a good ten miles before finding himself on the south bank of the river face to face with what he would call his garden of paradise on the Torrens.

A rising hill just back from the river would provide a perfect site for a house, and the surrounding land looked rich and productive. So Joseph went ahead and purchased a thirty-three-acre parcel of land and began work on the home of their dreams.

First he cut a sizeable shelter in the rock face – somewhere he could safely light a fire for winter warmth, somewhere he could sleep if he stayed overnight while building and somewhere he could feel safe from intruders. Then he dug out a large cellar and lined it with stones. It would keep his vegetables and other food fresh in the hot South Australian summers.

At last he could start on the house itself. This was the easiest part for Joseph, who was a carpenter by trade. He loved crafting wood, loved the feel of a smoothly planed surface and the tendrils of shavings that fell gracefully to the ground. It wasn't long before the walls of the lower storey were standing tall and proud.

Meanwhile, Lizzie looked after the children and the vegetable stall. In 1842, little Hannah was born, a sister for Harry and Georgiana. A pretty if somewhat sickly child, she never really thrived. Two months short of her fourth birthday, she contracted scarlet fever and died. Her parents were inconsolable until Lizzie suggested that they put her scuffed and muddy boots above the lintel over the back door of their new house as a memorial to her. With it they put a packet of seeds to represent new life. The effect on the family was astounding. Knowing that something of Hannah formed a part of their home allowed them the freedom to move on.

And life did go on for the Lindens. Lizzie went on to have six more children before she died in childbirth in 1856. Joseph finished the building, and called it Glengyle House. He then built a pub lower down the hill next to the bridge he had built over the Torrens some years before at the place they called Paradise. He was killed in an accident while driving his dray home from Adelaide one dark and moonless night in 1865, when his horse fell in a ditch while he was asleep at the reins.

*

Our retirement village with its Spanish inspired terracotta tiles is such a thing of wonder. The units sold quickly as we knew they would. We even arranged for my own mother to live there in her dotage. She is very happy in her serviced unit; she doesn't have to do more than boil the kettle for a cuppa and empty the cornflakes into her breakfast bowl. She especially likes the sunflowers that grow outside her window.

The Anniversary Gift

Jack was hoeing a trough in his vegie patch to plant seed potatoes, hoping that the wintry frosts of Cornwall had all but given up the ghost for the season. He noticed a circular piece of metal in the soil, covered in a crust of dirt that looked like it had been there for aeons. It was a wonder it glinted at all, but he noticed that in one place the dirty crust had dropped off. He put it in his pocket and went on working till lunchtime.

Jack gently cleaned the ring with a nail brush in the bathroom. It needed soaking so he left it in a glass until he'd finished his pasta. Then the dirt came off more easily, revealing two rings entwined together to form a single circle. They were gold in colour but a much earthier hue than his own wedding ring. And on the top was a dull blue stone, only crudely shaped and lacking lustre. He put it away among his socks in the drawer of the dresser, thinking that it might make a good present for Molly as their forty-fifth wedding anniversary was coming up.

He had recently googled appropriate gifts for a forty-fifth anniversary. Sapphires seemed to be the go. He found that sapphires symbolise the qualities required in a loving relationship, like loyalty, truth and reliability. Hmm, he mused. A gift of this jewel represents sincerity and faithfulness. Just perfect for the occasion.

He found a pretty blue velvet box at the local pound shop, and wrapped it and the sapphire in anniversary paper with blue irises on it, and tied it with a gold ribbon. With expectation shining in his eyes, he presented it to Molly at breakfast on the day.

Unfortunately, Molly was less than enchanted with her gift. 'It's far too small for my finger,' she grizzled. 'And look at this worthless-looking stone in it. Looks like a piece of old blue glass. What sort of present is this?'

Jack was devastated. He tried to explain the symbolism to Molly.

'That's all well and good,' she said, 'but I was hoping for a big box of chocolates like on previous wedding anniversaries.'

Still, Jack was intrigued by his rejected gift. He took it to the local jeweller to check it out.

'Bit dirty, isn't it?' Mr Jones exclaimed.

'I did clean it up,' protested Jack.

'You obviously didn't have the right tools, then,' was Mr Jones's reply. 'Here, let's have a go at it,' and he disappeared out to the back of his shop. Within a few minutes, he came back with the ring transformed. The gold glistened in a muted sort of a way, and the stone shone. 'I think it's a sapphire,' said the jeweller.

'I was hoping so,' was Jack's response.

'And this entwined pattern is consistent with something very old,' explained Mr Jones. 'I would guess that it's probably six or seven hundred years old, when such entwining was a common symbol of two lovers becoming one through betrothal. And the stone is certainly a sapphire. In those days, cutting sapphires into beautiful shapes wasn't yet thought of, and nor was there the technology to do much more than rumble stones in a revolving drum until they were reasonably smooth and reasonably round. Where did you get it?'

'In my back garden when I dug a trench for the potatoes.' Jack felt a bit sheepish at that point.

Mr Jones continued, 'It probably belonged to somebody who lived around here in about the fourteenth century. You could do some family history and trace back to whoever owned the land at that time.'

So Jack went back to Google and did just that, and found that in 1428 the land had been subdivided into tenement farms, one of which belonged to Jack's ancestor. Originally the land was owned by Andrew de Cardinham, who lived in the Penhallam manor, of which there were still some remains of the foundations and a moat in the woods nearby.

Jack could imagine the recently betrothed Andrew and Isolde, his svelte young lady, walking in the woods on a spring day such as today when there was just a touch of frost in the air, laughing at the birds and butterflies and stopping for a cuddle on a thick, soft bed of pine needles. One thing led to another, during which the ring fell from Isolde's slender finger. She didn't notice that it was missing until she got back to the manor. Returning to the scene, she searched high and low but couldn't find it again. What will Andrew say? she thought. We have probably lost the magic that comes with the ring. And so it seemed, for Isolde went on to have only one daughter, and her husband died early.

Next time Jack was in town, he called on the jeweller again. 'What do you reckon it's worth if I sold it?' he asked.

'I don't know for sure, but I think you could get in excess of £20,000 for it at auction.'

Jack's draw dropped in amazement. 'Say it again,' he said, not believing his own ears.

'I said £20,000. Not bad for a day's work, eh!'

Jack was sure that his gift might now be acceptable to Molly!

The Palace of Justice

Olive Whitaker began her job as clerical assistant at the Yarram Yarram Court House on 5 April 1939. There, in that octagonal red-brick building with its steeply pitched roof and stained-glass windows over the door that she walked through every working day, she answered the phone, typed letters for the lawyers, filed the correspondence and consigned out-of-date material to the archives in the basement.

It was on one of those days of working in the cold and airless basement that she happened across a file titled 'Peggy Whitaker: 1910'.

'Oh,' she said. 'Oh my goodness, same surname. I wonder what she did to cause her imprint to be left in this palace of justice.'

Olive knew that her grandparents Abraham and Margaret Whitaker had come to live on the outskirts of Yarram Yarram in 1885. They were both dead now, of course; their children had all moved away and Olive had lost touch with the other branches of her family. Although she knew that Abraham had originally been a farm labourer on some manorial property in Cheshire, had married and come to Australia with a wife, and had ended up owning a farm out on the soggy flats of the Tarra River here in Gippsland where together they had five children, she knew nothing at all of Margaret.

Who was she, where did she come from, who were her parents? The genealogical bug was getting to her. She wrote to Somerset House in London hoping that some lowly clerk would take down a dusty leather-bound volume that contained marriage details of the 1880s and look up the circumstances of Abraham's marriage.

It seemed months later that the marriage certificate arrived in its official airmail envelope. There, it was noted that in London in the first quarter of 1885 Abraham Whitaker, ag lab, aged 28, married Margaret Fitton, Galsworthy Hall, Cheshire, aged 20, daughter of Lord Charles Galsworthy.

'Lord Charles Galsworthy,' Olive gulped. 'Upper crust and all that.

How did Margaret descend the society ladder so quickly as to be amongst the poorest of the poor here in Yarram Yarram?'

In between pondering how to solve this next piece of the genealogical puzzle, she had work to do: phones to answer, letters to write, records to file and material to archive.

Next time Olive found herself in the basement of the court house, she withdrew the Whitaker file in order to surreptitiously take it back to her boarding room and have a good look, for perhaps Peggy Whitaker and Margaret Fitton of Galsworth were one and the same woman. Now, wouldn't that be something! Her boss kept her back late to finish urgent letters that had to catch the next morning's mail, so it wasn't until nearly nine o'clock that she had the chance to have a look.

She found the identity: Margaret Whitaker, alias Peggy Whitaker. 'So it was my grandmother after all. Well, I never!' She found the charge: larceny of valuable jewellery. She found the witness statement of the local jeweller: the woman came to his establishment and indicated that she wanted money in return for the jewellery.

'At first it looked like a set of garish costume jewellery,' he said, 'not worth much at all, but I took a closer look with the aid of my small but high-powered magnifying eyeglass. These were no fakes. No, they were the real thing.'

'Could you please describe the jewellery,' ordered the police prosecutor.

'In a lapis-blue velvet-covered box there was a pendant on a twenty-two-carat gold chain and a pair of earrings of similar design. They were made from small pearls of an extremely high lustre, set around an intricately patterned teardrop of lapis lazuli, with a gold edging. Very beautiful, if I may say so.'

'And quite valuable?' questioned the prosecutor.

'Yes, very valuable, I would say. I don't know where she would have stolen them from. Never seen them being worn in this district, and I have an eye for such things, you know.'

'I'm sure you do,' was the reply.

Next Olive read the defendant's statement.

'I swear on the Bible that I did not steal them. They are mine.'

Audible gasps of disbelief rose up and bounced back from the wooden carved ceiling of the court house.

'Could you explain how you came by them?' queried the prosecutor.

'My father gave them to me for my eighteenth birthday,' was the reply.

'And who is your father?'

'Charles Galsworthy. Lord Charles Galsworthy of Galsworth near Macclesfield in Cheshire in England.'

A strident cry of, 'Liar, liar pants on fire,' was heard from the gallery.

'The person in the gallery quoting William Blake will please desist. Or at least get your poetry right. "Deceiver, dissembler, your trousers are alight" sounds much more refined in a court of law such as this.'

General laughter ensued.

'Order in the court!' cried the clerk.

The judge turned to Abraham Whitaker. 'Were you aware that your wife owned such jewellery?'

'No, your Honour, I was not. Never seen it before in my life.'

Guilty was the verdict. Imprisonment for six months in the local prison was the sentence.

Now that was hardly a just verdict, thought Olive, to be given in this 'palace of justice'. Peggy didn't even get a right of reply. And that was hardly a fair sentence to be given in this 'palace of justice'. Who was going to look after her five children, two of whom were still very young, while she was incarcerated?

Olive slept only fitfully that windy night, her mind on Peggy and her pearls. Even the full moon ducking in and out of the strands of clouds looked like a giant pearl shining brightly in the deep black sky.

What if the jewellery was Peggy's after all? How could she find out?

During her lunch break the next day, Olive ran upstairs to the small legal library in the gallery of the palace of justice. Once before, she had seen a copy of *Burke's Landed Gentry* gathering dust on a shelf up there. Perhaps the Galsworthy family would be listed in there.

It was! And it mentioned an heirloom set of pearl jewellery that had been handed down through the family since the late Middle Ages. As eldest daughter, Margaret (Peggy) would have inherited it. So she was, after all, the rightful owner of the pearls. 'I just knew it in my bones,' whispered Olive. 'She was a good'un all the time.'

Now if this really is a 'palace of justice', the original sentence ought to be able to be overturned, she mused. And, book under her arm, she headed straight for the lawyer's office near her own desk. 'Is this evidence enough of Peggy's innocence?' she asked, showing Mr Johnson the page. 'Can we set justice straight again here, and if so, how?'

Old Mr Johnson took not even a second to reply in the affirmative. 'I remember the case,' he said, 'even though I was not involved.'

'Good, let's do it then,' said Olive. 'And I was also wondering where the pearls might be today. Would you happen to know?'

'As they weren't deemed to be Peggy's at the time, and the jeweller had no right to them, they should be stowed away somewhere in this building. Or perhaps in a strongbox at the bank down the road. I'll look into it, to keep you happy.'

'Actually I was wondering who might now be the legal owner?' Olive asked.

'Someone from the family, I presume,' was Mr Johnson's reply.

'But I'm not sure who's in the family any more. My parents both died in a car crash when they were quite young and we lost contact with Mum's siblings and cousins. Do you think you could make a case for me to have them?' she tentatively queried.

'I don't see why not,' he winked at her. 'I could look into that too.'

It was two weeks later when Mr Johnson stuck his head around her office door and said, 'Your court case is on tomorrow morning at 10 a.m. See you there.'

It was all over quite quickly. 'Granted. Case dismissed,' said the judge and handed Mr Johnson the small velvet box, which he opened and carefully took the pendant out and placed it round Olive's neck. 'Suits your beautiful red hair, just made for you,' he said, 'but I'll leave you to put on the earrings yourself. I'm not very practised in that art.'

Olive went to the mirror to admire her newly gotten treasure. 'Suits you, Olive Pearl Whitaker,' she whispered. 'My mother must have known something deep in her heart when she named me.'

She wondered where the pearls were between the eighteenth birthday celebration and the day of attempting to sell them. She wondered if there were any family papers that might reveal the secret. Maybe her mother had made a will. The Victorian Archives would have the answer to that. So she wrote to them.

Back came a copy of the will and an attached letter. 'I, Jean Whitaker of sound mind, do bequeath to my eldest daughter, Olive Pearl Whitaker, the pearl pendant and earrings that comprise the Galsworthy family inheritance.'

'Yes, yes, yes! They are mine,' she cried. 'I suppose when the will was initially read, I was too young to take it in. Now what light does this letter throw on the situation?'

'Olive, I want to tell you the story of these beautiful pearls,' her mother had written. 'Peggy told me that the year after she received them she eloped from Galsworthy Hall with Abe, her beloved farm hand, as her family wouldn't allow her to marry beneath her station. She took just a small bag with hardly anything in it. The jewellery case was hidden safely inside it. She never did tell Abraham about it. They went first to London, where they got married, then caught a steamer to Melbourne. In their cottage out at Tarra Creek, she found a loose brick in the chimney of the fireplace and hid the treasure in the wall cavity behind it. God knows what she thought she might do with it, but she said she was saving it for a rainy day, or perhaps a beautiful granddaughter.'

After months with very little food in the house, Peggy had come to her rainy day. She would sell the family jewels in order to survive. To think that it had come to that, Olive thought sadly.

Jet Star

Walter Holdsworthy worked in the jet factory in Whitby, sculpting the jewellery made so fashionable by Queen Victoria after the death of her Albert in 1861. For the rest of her life, the Queen always wore black to show the depths of her mourning. She particularly favoured black jewellery, and the best of black jewellery was made of jet at Whitby, a remote coastal town of Yorkshire. Many of her loyal subjects followed her example. So the factories at Whitby did a roaring trade.

Walter's fascination with the semi-precious fossilised wood began when he found pieces of jet along the beach at the foot of the rugged cliffs just north of Whitby where he liked to wander as a growing boy. It took him some years to learn to distinguish the dirty black pieces that were shale from those that would polish up into things of beauty. He patiently whittled the stubby pieces into all sorts of shapes with a sharp knife, and then polished them until they shone. At the factory, he became very skilled at creating beautiful pieces: pendants and necklaces, bracelets and earrings, all with some small accent of gold.

Walter made his beautiful Emilia a stunning necklace for her fiftieth birthday. A series of brightly shining black stars, bordered in gold, blazed on her neck. 'Oh my darling Emilia,' whispered Walter, 'You are so beautiful, you look like a queen.'

'I shall treasure this forever, dear Walter. It's gooder than gold.' She smiled coyly at him.

Some years later, the Holdsworthy family, with three teenage daughters now nearly all grown up, moved to Australia, settling in Adelaide, where Walter easily found employment in a jewellery business that specialised in crafting opal pieces.

The girls grew up and ironically all married men involved with gems and minerals in some form. Sarah married a Cornish copper miner and went to live in Wallaroo; Sophia wedded a grazier from Angepena in the

Flinders Ranges who had found gold on his property; and Susannah moved north to Broken Hill, where her husband assayed the ores of silver, lead and zinc mined there.

When their elderly parents had passed on, the starry jet necklace was bequeathed to the three daughters.

'How can we share one necklace?' the girls complained, until Susannah suggested, 'Why don't we divide the necklace into three portions so that each can have their section remodelled into some smaller pieces?'

'Good idea,' agreed the other two, and so it was.

Many years later, when Sarah, Sophia and Susannah's daughters came of age, each was presented with pieces made of the jet stars. Now the necklace had become ten smaller pieces. However, these granddaughters had no knowledge of the existence of their cousins, so dispersed and unconnected had the family become over the years.

In Adelaide in 1954, a new queen came to visit her subjects. Every schoolchild in South Australia was invited to the Wayville Showgrounds to attend a children's welcome for the recently crowned Queen Elizabeth II.

Three of Emilia's great grandchildren were chosen to be among the hundreds of primary school girls for the Wattle Dance. Their mothers had spent hours making the bright yellow dresses with their baubles of wattle around the hem and pretty yellow caps with pompoms on the top.

The families had come down from the country a few days before the occasion for rehearsals and all happened to stay at the CWA hostel in Kent Town, where the mothers had got to know each other over their breakfast cups of tea.

'For the big day, we all seem to have been rostered on duty at the same CWA tea stall. See you there,' said one of the mothers.

After discharging their Wattle girls into the capable hands of the dance coordinator, the three mothers arrived at the CWA tent. Dressed in their Sunday best, and unbeknown to the others, each woman arrived wearing her piece of Emilia's necklace.

'Oh my goodness!' exclaimed Audrey, who was rather stout, but her three-starred brooch looked fine pinned at collar level on her suit coat. 'We're all wearing similar jewellery. My brooch is made of jet. What about yours?' she questioned.

'The same,' uttered the other two in astonishment.

'A pendant star of Whitby jet,' said Coral, putting her hand to where the pendant was nestled between her tiny breasts on the salmon-pink fabric of her dress.

'And my starry earrings are too,' said Maxine, tossing her fiery mane to show them off. 'My mother told me that her grandfather Walter Holdsworthy made it back in the 1870s for his wife Emilia.'

'Mine too,' chorused the others. 'Then we must related, if we all had the same grandfather.'

'Eureka!' cried Coral. 'Pleased to meet you, dear relatives.'

And wouldn't you know it, as she drove past in her open black car, pinned to the pale blue coat that Queen Elizabeth was wearing with her pert little white hat was a black jet cabochon brooch set in a Celtic-patterned edging of gold.

'Sure to have been an heirloom from Queen Victoria,' laughed the three girls in unison.

For Whom Doth the Bell Toll?

Along the east coast of Suffolk lies a small and pleasant seaside village, where laughing children and their families come to stay in the balmy days of summer and to swim in the sea and play on the beach. They stay in holiday homes that follow a narrow line parallel to the coast. Dunwich, it is called. But in the middle ages Dunwich had been a large town, a bustling port, a commercial centre of some import.

However, the level of the sea began to rise and encroach insidiously onto the flat and boggy lands of the fens. In a huge storm in 1286, the town was flooded, not just water creeping in under the doorways, but covering whole buildings and drowning hundreds of good citizens. After the storm had abated, the sea level never did return to its old position. It kept eroding the flat and pebbly shoreline until nowadays only the thin line of houses remains.

Eight churches were among the buildings that found themselves at the bottom of the sea, eight churches each with solid and melodious bells. And every now and then when the sea is whipped up into a frenzy of crashing waves, people tell of hearing the bells again from beneath the waves, haunting muted sounds.

For whom did the bells toll?

Was a repeated single note rung on the bell at St Nicholas' to warn the people of the village that the Black Plague was among them? That devastating sickness that called courtesy of rats and their fleas, caused great tumours to ooze pus and turn black. Death was the only victor in the fight against it. St Nicholas' church was drowned in the fourteenth century.

Did the bell of St Bartholomew's toll for the earl, Thorkell the Tall? He and his wife Astrid lived in the Middle Ages in a crenellated castle at the top of the hill, and subjected his serfs to hard labour producing the wool that made him rich. Or perhaps the bell dinged its mournful dirge when their firstborn daughter failed to thrive and was buried in the churchyard. Or maybe a joyful peal rang out when their firstborn son, his heir apparent, was dunked in the font and held aloft for the congregation to admire his little naked body.

Did a whole carillon of bells ring out for the earl's son on the joyous occasion of his nuptials with the beautiful Guinevere? The entire neighbourhood danced in celebration on the village green, the girls garlanded in brightly coloured flowers, the boys with their brightest sashes flinging from their waists.

Was it for Thorkell's servant girl, his lover, who was stabbed with a kitchen knife by his jealous wife? No, not for her. Her burial was without ceremony down in the copse by the creek. Her sleek black cat continued to mew for her for months afterwards.

Did the Greyfriars bell ring out for the death of the abbot of the glorious Franciscan priory with its arched windows and ribbed ceilings? The abbot was poisoned by one of the earl's minions in the hope that the earl could take unto himself some of their large and fertile landholdings.

Was it for Bishop Felix, lately of Burgundy, who established Christianity in the Kingdom of the East Angles? His eloquent sermons in St Martin's turned the heart of many a good man away from his pagan roots. St Martins was lost to the sea early in the fifteenth century.

Did the ferocious wind sweep away the sound of the St Francis Chapel bell when it was rung to warn people asleep in their beds that the waters were rising and invading their homes? The sea eventually wiped out the chapel in the sixteenth century.

It possibly wasn't for the fisherman, Tom Holland, from the fleet, washed to his watery grave in a storm while far out to sea netting bream and conger eels. His wife and six children buried him from Katherine's chapel. Robbed of their breadwinner, they were forced to live in the workhouse for many long years until the oldest son married, and built a home to hold them all. The chapel and all the family were later covered by fathoms of water in the sixteenth century.

The bells of Blackfriars rang out in thanks when Henry III gifted the monastery with seven oak trees from the royal forests of Essex. But the bell was knocked to the ground with a great crashing when Henry VIII dissolved the priory. The abbot was hung for treason outside the magnificent gates when he refused to sign over the property to the king. Only the cockerel, standing on the fence post in the early morning, thrice crowed for the abbot. It was more than a century later that Blackfriars succumbed to the deep.

Most certainly the bells of All Saints tolled at the death of Queen Victoria, marking the end of her long, long reign. Relatively recently in 1922 the waters overtook the last remnants of this church.

Yea, for all of these the bells rang out, again and again. Doth the bell toll perhaps for thee…and for me?